Rāwhiti Island Medics

Welcome to Rāwhiti Island!

Sparks are set to fly with the arrival of new GP, single dad Owen—especially when he meets widow Carly. She's only on the island for a few more weeks, but she's promised to show him *everything* island life has to offer… Meanwhile, nurse Mia is navigating the challenges of being a single mum—and she's doing fine, honest! But when her little one's father lands back in her life, she faces her biggest challenge yet: telling him he has a daughter! Carly and Mia have put the idea of finding love behind them, but what will they do when it lands on their doorstep?

Meet the Rāwhiti Island Medics with…

Resisting the Single Dad Next Door

Available now!

And look out for Mia's story

Coming soon!

RESISTING THE SINGLE DAD NEXT DOOR

—

LOUISA GEORGE

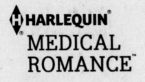

HARLEQUIN®
MEDICAL
ROMANCE™

Recycling programs
for this product may
not exist in your area.

ISBN-13: 978-1-335-73754-0

Resisting the Single Dad Next Door

Copyright © 2022 by Louisa George

For questions and comments about the quality of this book,
please contact us at CustomerService@Harlequin.com.

Harlequin Enterprises ULC
22 Adelaide St. West, 41st Floor
Toronto, Ontario M5H 4E3, Canada
www.Harlequin.com

Printed in U.S.A.

Award-winning author **Louisa George** has been an avid reader her whole life. In between chapters, she's managed to train as a nurse, marry her doctor hero and have two sons. Now she writes chapters of her own in the medical romance, contemporary romance and women's fiction genres. Louisa's books have variously been nominated for the coveted RITA® Award and the New Zealand Koru Award, and have been translated into twelve languages. She lives in Auckland, New Zealand.

Books by Louisa George

Harlequin Medical Romance

Royal Christmas at Seattle General
The Princess's Christmas Baby

SOS Docs
Saved by Their One-Night Baby

The Ultimate Christmas Gift
The Nurse's Special Delivery

Reunited by Their Secret Son
A Nurse to Heal His Heart
A Puppy and a Christmas Proposal
Nurse's One-Night Baby Surprise
ER Doc to Mistletoe Bride
Cornish Reunion with the Heart Doctor

Visit the Author Profile page
at Harlequin.com for more titles.

Praise for
Louisa George

CHAPTER ONE

TAP. TAP. TAP.

Owen Cooper opened an eye. Someone was tapping out a Morse code message in his bedroom.

Or was it a dream?

Tap. Tap. Tap-tap-tap.

He opened the other eye. A faint orange light from the rising sun partially lit the room, leaving corners still shrouded in darkness.

Dawn. Great. Add curtains to the shopping list.

Tap. Tap.

Not a dream.

Someone or something was in here with him. 'Mason?' he whispered. 'Mason, it's still night time. Go back to bed.'

Tap. Tap. Tap.

Not his son Mason—a dream. Which was a surprise, given he'd barely had any sleep.

The ferry had been late docking last night and there'd been no welcoming party for them on Rāwhiti Island's main pier. But he'd found an old, battered, red Jeep-style four-wheel drive at the end of the deserted pier with an envelope with his name on it stuck to the windscreen. It had contained an apology from the practice nurse, saying that they'd been busy, so hadn't been able to meet them, a set of keys and a hand-drawn map to his new house.

'New' meaning 'acquired for the first time', rather than 'recently built and unused'. Because this little house was well used—so used, in fact, that it needed bowling and completely rebuilding. And so not what he'd been led to expect when the island doctor job had been advertised as coming with accommodation.

There'd been no mention of Morse code messaging from his bedroom either.

He turned over, releasing a cloud of dust, and came face to face with two beady red eyes staring at him and a long grey beak.

He shot up and waved his hand. 'Hey! Get out!'

There was a flurry of feathers and a loud squawk. He managed to get a glimpse of caramel-brown feathers, something around the size of a hen, before it disappeared into the corridor.

A weka. One of New Zealand's flightless but feisty native birds. How the hell had that managed to get in? He lay back down on the old iron bed again, releasing another puff of dust, and mentally ran through his to-do list.

Secure the doors.

Clean the house.

Air his bed. Get a new bed.

Bird-proof his bedroom.

Reconsider his choices all over again, *ad infinitum*.

Had coming to this island twenty-two kilometres off the Auckland coast been a mistake? Uprooting his boy from everything familiar just so Owen could be the father he should have been all along? Everything familiar in the guise of Mason's mother had already left them and, he had to admit, left *him* floundering somewhat.

It was time to step up. It was long overdue.

But first…more sleep. He closed his eyes.

'Daddy?'

Okay, maybe not more sleep. He imbued his voice with a cheer he did not feel. 'Mason! Good morning.'

'Want Mummy.'

Owen's gut clenched like a tight fist. 'I know you do, buddy. How about we try to talk to her later on my tablet?' If she could fit her son into her busy schedule.

Mason's bottom lip wobbled and he nodded, blinking back tears. It sucked, just how brave his four-year-old was trying to be. 'There's a good boy. How did you sleep?'

His son scrambled up onto the bed and put his cheek against Owen's. 'The bed's all lumpy.'

He looked at his son in navy and white stripy pyjamas and his heart squeezed. 'I know, kid. I'm sorry. Mine is too. But it's only for a little while until your racing car bed arrives on the big boat. Did you see the weka?'

Mason's eyes grew huge as he nodded. 'He's my friend.'

The poor kid's world had been ripped apart by divorcing parents and a mother who'd decided she'd had enough of parenting, and generally being adult, and had left them so she could forge an acting career in the States. And now he was finding friends in the local fauna. Was that a sign of emotional damage, or resilience and resourcefulness? 'He's a bit skitty for a friend. When you start kindy on Monday, there'll be loads of other children to play with.'

A nod. 'Can we go fishing now?'

'Later. We've got so many jobs to do first.'

There came a pout reminiscent of his mother's dramatic talent. 'Fishing first? Please.'

'No, Mason. We've got too much to do.'

The pout hardened into a sulk. 'You said fishing.'

He had. Last night, as they'd hauled their suitcases across the dirt from car to house, they'd passed a little tinny boat moored off the end of the property's jetty and Owen had promised Mason that fishing would be high on the agenda of their *Boy's Own* adventures.

What was the harm if they ignored all the chores and started the adventures ASAP? There was no one to tell him not to. No one they had to report progress to. No one else to take into account. It was just Mason, him and two whole days before the job started.

He could either clean the house now or later. The dust wasn't going anywhere. So why not spend some time with his boy before diving into chores?

The harm was that it had been fifteen years since he'd taken a boat out onto the water and he wasn't prepared. But, after a bit of detective work, he found some dusty fishing rods propped up in the shed. And, luckily, the newest things provided in his accommodation were life jackets in assorted adult's and children's sizes hanging up in the porch.

After securing one on himself and one on his son, he gathered up the ancient fishing rods and lures and then pushed the little four-and-a-half-metre aluminium boat out into the calm water and they hopped in. There was even petrol in the outboard motor. 'Hey, we're in business, Mason! Whoever lived here before us clearly paid far more attention to boating than the living quarters.'

Having cranked up the motor, he steered the tin boat out from their cove and turned right. There was probably a proper name for the direction they were heading in, but he couldn't remember. From this vantage point, he could see the contours of the island stretching out ahead and above. Undulating hills were covered in dense, natural bush of kanuka, manuka, beech trees and assorted ferns. He pointed out tui birds and fantails. 'The Te Reo Maori name for those little fantails is *piwakawaka*.'

'Piwaka...?' His mini-me echoed and grinned.

'Almost. Good effort.' Owen looked at the bush and sighed, hoping he'd made the right decision to come here. It was a far cry from their modern suburban house on the edge of the city and close to the motorway.

Here, housing was sparse, but a range of old villas, crumbling holiday homes and new architecturally sophisticated buildings dotted the hillsides, each with its own private path down to the golden beaches and coves. Numerous jetties jutted out into the calm turquoise water.

Owen tried to remember the things his grandfather had taught him about fishing, quieted the engine, attached the lures to the line and cast them into the sea. But soon all fishing was forgotten as Owen made out shapes scudding through the water towards them.

'See the dolphins, Mason? Look!' He lifted the boy onto his lap and pointed to the silvery shapes jumping out of the water. 'Wow. Look at that. They're doing acrobatics.'

Mason's hesitant smile grew as he watched the beautiful creatures splash ahead of them, tumbling and turning. Then his boy started to laugh, a full, gurgling, belly laugh that Owen couldn't remember having heard for a very long time. He took a huge, deep breath and let it out slowly. Okay, so despite the early-morning bird alarm clock, the fact his accommodation was falling apart and that his son still wasn't convinced he was going to survive without his mama, moving here had been a good decision after all.

The dolphins swam faster and faster ahead of them, and Owen quickly pulled in the fishing lines, cranked up the outboard motor and followed them, struggling to juggle the steering, but managing his son's safety and laughing along for the first time in far too long.

Over on shore he saw a woman in a cove frantically waving her arms at him. He waved back, then realised she was beckoning to him, so he slowed the boat down and steered towards the property's little jetty.

As he closed in, he could see she was around

medium height. Young…at least, a few years younger than his thirty-two, maybe. He wasn't the best judge of women's ages these days. Or women in general, it seemed, given his failed marriage.

She was wearing a zipped-up navy wetsuit top and short black shorts. Bare feet. Tanned. Bloody great legs. Strawberry-blonde hair scraped back into a tight ponytail. Behind her and nestled into the bush was a small collection of wooden buildings, and to her right was a large playground complete with swings and slides. To her left, a huge boat shed housed a lot of bright orange kayaks and little Optimist boats and, maybe a hundred feet beyond the boat shed, was a cute cream-coloured cottage that looked in a lot better repair than his.

Attached to the small jetty he noticed a sign.

Camp Rāwhiti
Outdoor education specialists
For Sale

Ah, he'd been told in his interview that part of his remit would be to offer medical advice and assistance to a school camp place. Maybe this was it. Or wouldn't be for much longer, given it was for sale. He cut the engine and moored the boat onto a cleat.

Then he tried to find his best smile for the scowling woman in front of him.

Carly Edwards was sick of the careless weekend island visitors' total disregard for safety and serenity. But she was surprised the man in the boat, who seemed older than she'd first assumed—mid-thirties—had a small child with him. Certainly, he should have been setting a better example.

When he stepped off his little boat, she dashed over to the jetty and couldn't help railing at him. 'Just exactly what the hell do you think you're doing? Can't you see there are children here?'

He frowned as he looked over at her stand-up paddle-board class in the shallow water. 'I wasn't anywhere near them.'

'Not yet, but I had no way of knowing if you had control of your vessel. And you were going far too quickly.'

'I can assure you, I wasn't.' Dark eyes glittered in anger. 'I was in full control.'

'The wash is enough to make them feel seasick. We're on island time here. Slow down.'

He glanced down at his son and then back at her, clearly not wanting to argue in front of the boy. His eyes were a deep, dark brown, like his hair, which was slicked back with a clipped fade at the sides—very 'city'. His skin was smooth, clean-shaven and pale, as if he spent a lot of time indoors. His clothes were typical weekender. Pale blue polo shirt and sand-coloured cotton shorts. He filled them very nicely. She could be objective about that. He had strong-looking arms, she'd noticed as he'd tied the rope, and a body that looked used to exercise. But there was one thing that surprised her—he wore jandals on his feet rather than boat shoes. A mistake in her assumptions there—usually, the city people wore new boating shoes.

'We'll just have to agree to disagree.' He bristled, his jaw set. 'I'll make sure to keep an eye on my speed in future.'

If it was meant as an apology, it lacked the basics, such as the words *I'm sorry*. But she guessed it was all she was going to get. 'Thank you.'

'Mason hasn't seen dolphins before, and we were following them.'

As excuses went, she had to admit it was a good one. The dolphins out here were so enchanting and friendly, and they liked to show off their tumbling skills. She knew how spellbinding they were. Even so, shaking her head and trying to control her frustration, she turned and walked to the edge of the water, scanning to count her class in. All present and correct.

'Okay, everyone. Come in. Time's up,' she shouted. 'Bring the SUPs out of the water and load them back on the racks, please. You know the drill.'

Behind her the little boy asked, 'Daddy, can I play on the swings?'

'I don't think so. The scary lady might tell us off. Again. We should go.'

Scary lady. Was that what she was now? She really hoped not. But there was humour in his tone and it was infectious. She pressed her lips together to stop a smile escaping. Speeding was no laughing matter.

'But, Daddy…*pleeease.*'

Despite the longest 'please' she'd ever heard, the little guy's voice was tentative, almost re-signed to a negative response.

And it came. 'I'm sorry, son. I promise we'll fix up the garden and I'll build you a playground as soon as we can get the supplies sent over.'

So, he was a new resident of the island. He could have bought any one of the houses for sale recently.

It was none of her business. Her business was here, these children in the lesson. This camp. But not for much longer. Someone would come and buy the place and she wouldn't be the warden of the cove—tempering visitors' enthusiasm and speed and protecting the sanctity of the place. She'd be off exploring the world beyond Rāwhiti

Island, trying to forget the heartache and shake off the sting of bittersweet memories.

'Today?' Hope resonated in the little boy's tone.

'No, buddy. It's going to take a bit longer to build a playground.'

'Okay, Dad.'

Scary lady. She turned and watched the boy's eyes look greedily at her playground as they started to climb back into the boat. Poor kid. 'Hey, bud. What's your name?'

He looked up at her with eyes as dark as his father's. 'Mason.'

'Well, Mason, you can play in my playground if you want, as long as Daddy promises to enrol in a day skipper class.'

The boy's head whipped round to look up at his father. 'Daddy?'

The man shot her a look that was filled with shock, and possibly anger. He held her gaze for a moment and she steeled herself for whatever he was about to throw at her—that he was a skilled boatsman and how dared she suggest such a thing?

But his shoulders dropped, as if he was consciously making himself stay calm, and he gave her a sharp nod. 'Okay. Yes, Mason, go and play. Five minutes. Then we have to go back to do the list of jobs we're avoiding.'

She could relate to that at least. 'Excellent. They run the courses at the Coastguard offices in Auckland, or if you're here for any length of time you can do them at the yacht club. Or on-line.' How to ask if someone lived here without asking if they lived here? But he just gave another nod. 'I'll look into it.'

'Tell them Carly sent you. Should get a dis-count.'

'Thanks...um... Carly.' He looked down at his feet then back at her. 'Your accent is English, is that right?'

'Sure is.' She didn't have to explain anything.

The man nodded as if he understood her re-luctance to have a conversation. 'Well, thanks again. It's been a difficult time. He'll love just being able to play.'

His eyes were deep and soulful. For a beat she was spellbound by the flecks of gold in his irises, and simultaneously her heart crushed to hear of the boy's struggles. Which was a heady combina-tion—she knew exactly how it was to deal with difficult things and she certainly didn't wish that on a little one.

But she could not want to know why things had been difficult or why they were here. She could not want to know anything more about them, no matter how curious she was. Or how good-looking this man was. She was drawing a line under this place, finally, after her own very difficult time.

'Talking of jobs…' She returned his nod with one of her own, then turned and walked away back to her class and her home…for now.

Above all, she didn't have time to stand around looking into any man's eyes. Especially one who'd put her class's lives at risk. She wasn't going to give him a chance to risk her heart too.

CHAPTER TWO

'THE ISLAND POPULATION is around five hundred and sixty now—we've had a huge growth spurt with the new development round at South Cove. But that number easily quadruples, and more, in the summer with holidaymakers, day-trippers and boat races swelling the numbers.' Mia, the nurse practitioner, put a tray of steaming mugs of tea down on the white plastic table in the surgery staff's lunch-cum-meeting room. 'Although, we have such a great microclimate here, we have visitors all year round. Have you been to the island before?'

Owen shook his head. 'I tried to get over a couple of times, but the trips were cancelled because of lockdowns. I even interviewed online.'

'Thank goodness those lockdowns are well and truly in the past. So, it's your first time here.' She clapped her hands. 'Oh, you'll love it. Everyone's so friendly. It's such a happy community.'

Apart from the scary lady, clearly.

It had taken the best part of their boat journey

home for Owen to get over the grumpy way she'd spoken to them. Although, she had let Mason play on the swings—her one redeeming feature. Not counting the amazing legs and pretty face, obviously. Hopefully, their paths wouldn't cross again.

He realised Mia was staring at him, waiting for a response. Not wanting to let her know he hadn't been listening, he cleared his throat and put the grumpy woman out of his head. 'It's definitely different to the city practice. We were rushed off our feet all day, every day.'

'Then you'll soon start to enjoy this slower pace of life.' Mia nodded.

'I already am.' It had been a busy morning, trying to get Mason ready for kindergarten and then getting himself into work on time, so Owen was relieved they'd closed his appointment template for the day so he could orientate to the computer booking system and get to know the staff and routine. Now it was lunchtime already, and the time had flown by.

'We have appointment slots every morning. Monday to Friday.' Anahera, the elderly receptionist, put a large plate of raspberry lamingtons on the table, then sat down across from him. 'Then you're free to do paperwork and home visits if necessary.'

'Home visits? Not something we did in the city.'

'We have a very different approach here. Much more of a community feel. We help each other out.' Anahera picked up the plate and offered it to him. 'Please, take one. Take two. You'll be doing my waistline a favour. And you'll be on call every alternate day, just for emergencies. Mia's on call the other days. You'll get the hang of it all.'

And that was the team. Him, a nurse practitioner and a receptionist. No handy X-ray machine. Blood tests were sent by the last ferry every day. But at least the results came back via email, and there was a small pharmacy on the island that doubled up as a souvenir shop. It seemed every business here did double duty. The yacht club was also the postal service, and the tiny supermarket did takeaway hot food.

He took a bite of the bright pink cake covered in coconut and sighed at the pillowy softness and sweet fruity flavour. 'I could get used to lunch like this every day.'

'Only for special occasions. But we like to think most days on Rāwhiti are special, eh, Mia?' Anahera winked at the nurse.

'I'm all for that.' Owen laughed and kept his thoughts about healthy eating to himself. 'At the interview I was told I'd have babysitting back-up if I needed it.'

Anahera grinned. 'That'll be me. I can come over any time at all. I've had six of my own and have three grand-babies. That's why I wasn't here on Friday to welcome you. I had to go to the mainland to see my newest. A wee preemie. Wasn't due for another six weeks and took us all by surprise. We had a mad dash to get my daughter over to hospital before little Aroha made her dramatic entrance.'

'Congratulations.'

'And I was dealing with an asthmatic who needed an urgent evac to City hospital,' Mia added. 'We've had a run on evacs recently. Sometimes we can go for weeks without anything, then we get a rush on.' She smiled apologetically. 'I'm sorry no one was there for the big welcome. I hope we're making up for it now?'

'It was fine—' He was interrupted mid-speech as the door was flung open.

'Anahera! Mia! Anyone home…? Yoo-hoo! Oh.'

Oh, indeed.

The scary lady from the school camp was standing in the doorway, breathless, her pony-tailed hair dishevelled. She had a faded yellow T-shirt on today and a pair of denim cut-off shorts above those gorgeous, toned legs. He drew his gaze up to her eyes. She glared intense brown back at him.

'What's up?' Mia jumped up. 'Got a problem?'

'Not until now.' Carly's fixed stare on Owen

grew into a smile the moment she looked at the younger woman. 'I was just grabbing some things from the shop and remembered I need some extra supplies of EpiPens and Steri-strips until my order comes through from the wholesalers.'

Anahera stood up. 'Sure thing, honey.' Then the receptionist turned to Owen before going into the back supply room. 'Dr Owen Cooper, this is Carly from the island outdoor camp. Our designated first responder in the event of any major incident. We all take orders from her then.'

He imagined she'd be very good at bossing people around in the event of an emergency and, from his experience, just for breathing or enjoying the outdoors on a boat.

'*Dr* Cooper?' Carly pressed her lips together as her eyebrows rose. He sensed her surprise wasn't exactly positive. 'Signed up for the class yet?'

'You're going to do paddle-board lessons?' Mia laughed. 'That was quick work.'

Carly just frowned. 'Day skipper lessons. Crucial for round here, don't you think?'

Mia's gaze slid from Carly to Owen. Her eyes narrowed. 'What's going on? What am I missing?'

Carly shrugged. 'Just trying to keep everyone safe.'

'Okay.' The nurse frowned suspiciously at them both and then hauled a large bag onto her shoulder. 'I'll leave you two to whatever it is that you're not telling me. I've got to pop over to kindy and drop off Harper's lunch. Silly me left it in my bag. Then I'm popping over to do Winnie's dressings and to check in with Nicky Clarke. She's not due for another couple of months, but after last week's preemie adventures I'm not taking any chances.'

Call him a coward, but Owen nearly yelled at Mia to take him with her. Instead, he stood up and put his hand out to the camp woman. 'Hello. We should probably have done this on Saturday, but hi, I'm Owen. New doctor.'

She fitted her hand into his and shook tightly. Her eyes sparked and glittered. He got the feeling she was irritated and amused by him, or by the situation, and he had no idea why. 'Carly Edwards. Although, I think you probably gathered that the other day.'

No 'pleased to meet you' or other niceties.

He let his hand drop from hers but not before noticing her warm, soft skin and assured grip. 'So, we're going to be working together.'

'Only in an emergency.' Her gaze caught his and held.

He got the message loud and clear. *Back off. We're not as friendly as we say we are here on Rāwhiti Island.*

'And the camp's up for sale?'

'Yes.'

'So, will it still be a school camp when it's sold?'

'That depends on the new owner.' A frown settled again across her forehead. 'Why?'

'Just interested in what my new neighbours are likely to be doing.'

'A lot of the bush on the property is covenanted so they won't be able to change that. But I suppose they'll have free rein to do what they like with the buildings. Develop the whole place, probably, but we're trying to find a buyer who'll keep it as a camp first and foremost.'

'We?'

'Me and Mia.' Carly nodded towards the spot where Mia had stood moments before. He detected a frisson of pride tinged with something else. Her demeanour softened and she smiled, almost sadly. There was clearly a lot more to this story. 'We own the camp.'

Oh. Not what he'd expected, although he wasn't sure what he'd expected…a husband-and-wife team perhaps? Plus, Mia was a New Zealander, and Carly very definitely had an English accent. 'Right. Okay. So, are you two married or something?'

Carly's eyes nearly bugged out of her head and she spluttered on a chuckle. 'Something, yes. We're sisters-in-law.'

But so far no husbands mentioned or seen…
'And Mia lives at the camp too?'

'No. She and her little one have their own place just round the corner, near the marina. A few houses along from the yacht club.'

'I haven't ventured along there yet.'

'You should. Wiremu does a good pint.' She gave him a stiff smile that he chose to decipher as polite friendliness. Then, 'But, anyway, I doubt that whatever the new owners do will make much difference to you. There's a hill between us.'

There's a lot more than that.

He was trying to work out the jigsaw puzzle of her life. Although, why, he didn't know. First, it was none of his business. Second, he knew from his own experience just how complicated families could be. Third, he had a sneaky suspicion that his interest had a lot to do with her spark and bite. And he could not pursue that. 'What will do when you sell up?'

'Travel.' A curt nod. She was forthright but not gushy. 'There's a lot of world to see beyond Rāwhiti Island.'

'And your husbands…?'

The door swung open again and a portly old man staggered in. 'Carly!' he managed. 'Thank God.'

His words were slurred and his movements sluggish. Then he clutched the doorframe, his knuckles white with the effort. His lips worked but no more words came out. His face drooped like molten wax on one side, then he slumped forward.

Everything else forgotten, Owen jumped up and caught the man before he slid to the floor. 'Let's get him onto the examination couch. My room's closer.'

'Sure.' Carly took the other side, ducking under the man's underarm and holding him up with her shoulder. Together, they manoeuvred him out and across the small waiting room and into Owen's consultation room, where they propped him up against the couch. He slumped heavily to one side, as if he couldn't hold that part of himself upright.

Carly swung the man's legs up and they laid him back on the couch, a pillow under his back and head. 'Wiremu,' she said gently but with authority. 'Wiremu, can you tell me what's happening to you? Do you have any pain?'

Wiremu. She'd mentioned that name only a moment ago. Owen slipped a pulse oximeter onto Wiremu's finger then grabbed the sphygmomanometer and started to take the man's blood pressure.

Anahera bustled into the room, arms full of packages. She stopped short as she recognised the man on the couch. 'I wasn't sure where you'd got to, but I heard voices. Wiremu? Oh, Wiremu.' She glanced worriedly from Owen to Carly and dropped the packages onto the desk. 'What's happening? What is it?'

'Looks like a stroke, but we can't be sure. His oxygen levels are okay, but his blood pressure is very high.' Owen fitted his fingers into Wiremu's clenched fist. 'Wiremu, can you squeeze my hand?'

The man blinked up at them but said nothing. He squeezed Owen's fingers well with his left hand, but didn't seem to register that he had a right side at all.

Anahera fluttered next to them. The capable, calm woman of before had gone and been replaced with worry. 'What do we do? Can't you give him something? A blood thinner?'

'I don't know if it's a clot or a bleed, Anahera. If I give him the wrong treatment, we could make him worse. We need to get him to hospital as soon as we can and get some scans done of his brain.' It occurred to him then that everyone knew each other here. Perhaps this man was a relative. 'Do you have details of his next of kin? Family?'

Anahera's eyes filled with tears. 'He's my brother.' She patted Wiremu's hand. '*Ae*, boy? My little brother. And we're going to sort you out.'

Carly had the satellite phone in her hand. She was calm, clear and concise, showing no emotion at all and anticipating exactly what Owen had been about to ask her to do. 'I'm through to ambulance control. They're dispatching a helicopter immediately and need some more medical information.'

She passed the phone to Owen for medical details. 'Suspected CVA. Right hemiplegia. Dysphasia. Hypertensive at two hundred and four over one hundred. Needs urgent admission.'

A crackle and then, 'On our way, Doc. Over and out.'

'How long?'

'Twenty minutes, usually.' Carly took the phone from him and hung up. 'There's a helicopter landing pad behind the yacht club. Three minutes away.'

Owen did another round of observations on Wiremu, and tried to engage him in conversation so he could assess his mental and consciousness state, but it was clear he was deteriorating fast.

'Anahera, go tell Lissy what's happening. She's going to need support, especially with those grand-babies staying with her too. Someone's going to have to go to the hospital.' Carly wrapped her arms around the older woman and hugged her tightly. 'I'll let Mia know what's happened. Go be with your family.'

'It's okay. I'll call her.' The older lady's eyes

slid to Owen with regret and sadness. 'I don't want to leave the new doctor on his first day.'

Amazed at the dedication of his little team, Owen shook his head. 'Hey, I can absolutely manage. Go. Please.'

He wasn't sure exactly how he would answer the phones and simultaneously tend to the patients on his own if Mia was going to be out on calls, but he'd do it.

'Thank you.' Carly managed a soft smile as she glanced at him, and for a moment he felt wildly happy that he'd made her smile, as if he'd achieved some small victory and put a crack in her armour.

She walked Anahera to the door. 'Yes, go now. You have to prioritise yourself and your family. I'll put something on the *whanau* chat group. There'll be food in your freezers by this evening. Anything else you need?'

Anahera shrugged. 'I don't know.'

'When you've had a chance to think, let me know.'

'I can't believe this is happening on the heels of Friday's hospital dash.' The receptionist put her hand on Carly's arm. 'Thanks, love.'

'Hey. You did so much for me. You do it for everyone else.' Carly watched her go and exhaled. 'She's always the first to help others but can't accept it for herself.'

The *whanau* chat group—'family' chat group? 'She's your family? Wiremu's your relative? You should have said.'

'Not blood family. But we're all close. You can't not be, living in a place like this. Mia's my family. She grew up here and they all adopted me when I arrived. Didn't you, Wiremu?' She stroked their patient's hand, picking it up and examining it, and he could see her eyes glittered with tears.

You did so much for me. Carly had said that to Anahera.

More questions stacked up in his head. What was her story? She was calm and controlled, guarded and forthright. And yet when she'd held Anahera, and now with Wiremu, there was a gentleness and caring he hadn't expected.

And now, close up, he could see things he hadn't noticed before too. There was no wedding ring on her slender fingers. No rings at all, in fact. No jewellery, apart from silver studs in her ears. Her hair had strands of red and gold running through it. She had more freckles than he could count running across her nose and kissing her cheeks.

Kissing…

His eyes darted to her sensuous mouth and he dragged them away. It was so inappropriate to think like that.

What the hell was wrong with him?

She lifted her head and caught him looking at her. But, instead of berating him as he expected, she nodded. The smile she gave him was almost friendly. 'Thanks for the help, Doc.'

She was thanking him? And yet hadn't he been told she held higher ranking in an emergency? 'Carly, do you mind if I ask…are you medically trained?'

'I've got advanced first aid training and fire training, plus logistics and civil defence. Which means that if anything happens on this island, be it medical, fire, tsunami or other emergency, I have to deal with it, then send for help. We've got emergency response jet-skis to get to any emergency faster, be it on land or sea. The roads here don't go to every house, and they're gravel and winding, so sometimes travelling by sea is quicker. I attend first, assess and then get help. It works for most things. Although, we're grateful to have a doctor here now. First permanent one we've ever had.'

'Why now and not before?'

'We couldn't get anyone to fund a doctor, so we raised money for the medical centre, which has always been nurse-led. But with the population growing we needed more. Poor Mia can't be on call twenty-four-seven, especially with a toddler. We put a case to the health board and they finally agreed to partially funding a GP role. The other funds come from us, the users, just like on the mainland. So here you are.'

Here he was. Wondering how he was going to fit in to such a close-knit community. Would they have room for him in their hearts too and, more importantly, space for his son?

He realised Carly was looking at him with a puzzled expression.

She tugged at his arm and walked him a little away from their patient. 'Is he going to be okay?'

He made sure they were out of Wiremu's earshot. 'With a stroke patient it's imperative to get them help immediately, before too much damage has been done, and I'm hoping we're doing that. You did well to stay so calm, given you know him. A lot of people would have panicked.'

She exhaled deeply, sticking her hands into her denim shorts pockets. 'I deal with hundreds of kids in my job. They provide enough drama and hysterics, closely followed by the parent helpers. I've learnt not to get emotionally involved.'

He wondered, briefly, whether she meant just in her job or in her private life too. And it occurred to him that she hadn't answered his question about husbands living at the camp. But now wasn't the time to go back to that conversation.

He hadn't come here to get involved with another woman. He was here for his son and that was all.

And then the sound of chopper blades rent the air and the only person in his head was Wiremu.

CHAPTER THREE

CARLY HID HER face from the sandblasting caused by the updraft of the helicopter as it rose above the bay into the clear summer sky. Then she turned and walked back towards the medical centre to collect her supplies.

The new doctor strode purposefully ahead of her, in a hurry to get back to the surgery. She had to admit he was impressive. Not just in looks, but in his demeanour too. In the aftermath of an emergency, people often crumbled, but he seemed just as level-headed now as before. But then, he hadn't known Wiremu for years, the way she and Anahera had.

Or maybe he was always like that...calm and considered. Except on Saturday when she'd growled at him and he'd clearly fought to keep his temper at bay. Which meant there was more to him than he liked to portray...hidden depths. *Stop it.*

She did not want to know what was going on behind his professional exterior.

The emergency bleeper on her shorts belt started to vibrate against her waist. Now what? There was still so much she had to do to get ready for the influx of children tomorrow morning. She looked at the message coming through.

Emergency. Bream Bay. Fallen tree. Simon injured his leg.

Okay. Everything else had to wait.

Taking a deep breath, she called out, 'Hey, Doc! Owen?'

He stopped short and turned to her, his dark eyes roaming her face. *God*, he was lovely to look at. 'Yes?'

'Don't get too comfortable, we're needed out at Bream Bay.'

He gave a slight frown, more curiosity than irritation. 'Do you have any details?'

'There's been an accident. Not quite sure what we're going to find, but apparently a tree has fallen on someone.'

His eyebrows rose. 'Wow. Okay. We'd better get going. Good job I don't have any patients booked in.'

He must have been feeling overwhelmed, especially with his receptionist gone now. 'It gets like this sometimes, but people do understand if you run late. They realise if it's an emergency then it's likely to be someone they know, and usually want to help out too.' She pulled out her phone and sent a text to Mia. 'I've just let Mia know what's happening. The surgery phone has an answer-machine, so don't worry about missing anything. You can follow up when we get back.'

He nodded. 'Of course. Do you have everything, or do I need to grab emergency supplies?'

'I've got a full first aid bag down at the marina.'

'Okay.' He unlocked the surgery door. 'I'll just grab my work bag, put the closed sign up and lock everything up.'

She stood in the open doorway. 'Have you got any swimwear with you?'

'No. Why?'

'It's jet-ski time.' Her gaze slid over his body… purely for sizing purposes. At least, that was what she told herself. She was not checking out the man's body. She was not noticing the broad shoulders or the nice backside. She was not thinking about what was under his neat white shirt and grey chinos. 'We'll grab some togs from the pharmacy. They sell stuff like that for the tourists.'

He nodded. 'I'll remember to bring some to work in future. I just expected I'd be in the clinic all day.'

'You usually will be, but best to have a bag of swim stuff close by for emergencies. I'll meet you down at the marina. Just along that road.' She pointed out of the surgery window. 'Orange jet-ski on the floating dock. I'll get it ready to go and grab the first aid kit from the locker while you get changed.'

'Give me two minutes.' He dashed into the pharmacy while she ran to the quay.

He was by her side in no time, wearing a black rash vest that hugged his toned body, navy-and-white-striped swim shorts and jandals. A pair of trainers was slung over his shoulders, hanging by the laces. His dark hair was mussed-up, presumably from pulling his clothes over his head. He looked, quite simply, gorgeous.

Then she gave herself a good talking to. Just because a man was gorgeous didn't mean anything. Just because, despite her first impressions, he was actually quite nice, calm and controlled in an emergency, had a cute, dimpled smile and showed compassion to his co-workers, didn't mean a single thing.

Not. A. Thing.

But she did quietly thank her lucky stars that the new doctor wasn't averse to adventure. Although, she'd realised that when she'd watched him zoom across the cove in pursuit of dolphins with his little boy.

And, far too quickly, questions began to crowd her head. Where was the mother of his child? Why were just father and son here? What had made him come to the island when, by all accounts—background info from Mia, mainly—he'd had a perfectly successful city practice?

She brushed those thoughts away and gunned the jet-ski engine, then threw a life jacket to him. 'Put this on. Hop on. And hold on.'

'Got you.' He slid the jacket on, pulling it tight across his chest, and then slipped his messenger-style work bag across his body.

She was aware of the slide of his legs against hers as he straddled the jet-ski. She was aware of the warm stretch of his hands at her waist and his scent of anti-perspirant—something minty and very definitely male.

Acutely aware…as if someone had flicked a switch inside her. A switch that hadn't been working for three long years. Hell, she hadn't wanted it to work ever again, but now, with his hands round her waist, she felt jittery and off-balance.

How long since she'd been held? Kissed? Cared for? Her chest hurt at the thought of what she'd lost. So much. So many plans, hopes and dreams with the man she'd loved had been cruelly snatched away from her in a freak accident. It hit her that what she missed most was human contact. The little, everyday affections. Someone to ask how her day had gone. Someone to hold. Someone to hold her.

And why was she having these thoughts right now? And around Dr Owen Cooper? A few weeks before she was leaving?

She lifted her chin, felt the spray refresh her cheeks and wipe away the sadness she'd thought she'd come to terms with. Had come to live with. But, she realised, it was an unwanted talisman she carried everywhere, tainting everything, every thought, every plan.

Which was why she needed to leave this place to create some new memories and find out who she was, now she no longer fitted the description of wife or daughter-in-law.

Soon enough they were at Bream Cove, where Simon's wife, Michaela, was frantically waving. After securing the jet-ski to the jetty, Carly waited for the woman to fill her in.

'Carly, thank God. He's out the back of the house. He was supposed to be trimming the lower branches, but the old idiot got carried away without thinking it through.'

They raced up the jetty, along the gravel path and out into the paddock behind the old cottage where tall, thick podocarp trees provided a natural barrier between workable land and bush. Carly scanned as she ran and eventually made out a figure pinned underneath a large branch that must have spanned almost half a metre wide.

'There! Quick.' She turned, expecting Owen

to be somewhere behind her, but he was at her side, now overtaking her, covering the distance in no time. Somehow, he'd managed to put his trainers on—a good move, given the thistles and clumps of sedge grasses that scratched her ankles and feet.

'Crush injury. We need another helicopter. Quick.' Without even having to assess too closely, Owen clearly knew this was urgent as he knelt next to the man's head. 'Hey, Simon. I'm Owen, the new doctor. We're going to get this branch off your leg and see how much damage you've done.'

'Hurts.' Simon grimaced and tried to sit up.

'I know. Try to keep still, mate.' Owen put his hand on the man's chest and gently encouraged him to lie back down. 'We'll sort you out. I just need to make sure you haven't done any damage to your back or neck before we move either you or the tree.' After assessing for any other injuries, Owen turned to Michaela, calm and totally in control. 'When did this happen?'

She shrugged, her face pale, her fingers knotted in the hem of her T-shirt. 'To be honest, I don't know. Could be half an hour. Could be two hours. I was out on the boat for a while, then pottering in the kitchen.'

He turned to Carly and nodded. 'We need to be careful when we get the pressure off his leg.'

'Crush syndrome?'

'Yes, although it's his leg that's trapped, not his torso, so I'm not expecting it. But we don't know how long he's been here, or how much toxin build-up there could be, so we need to be careful and watch for signs.' He slipped a pulse oximeter onto Simon's finger. 'I'm just going to see what your oxygen levels are, and I'll give you some pain relief. Then we'll get that log off your leg.'

Simon groaned. 'Thanks... Doc.'

Carly dialled up the satellite phone, got through to ambulance control, and gave all the details of the injury and the location of the nearest helicopter landing pad, which, luckily, was at a neighbouring property only a few minutes away.

Owen pulled the small portable oxygen cylinder from the first aid kit, fitted it to a mask then slid it over Simon's head. Then he pulled out some ampoules, drew liquid into a syringe and jabbed Simon's arm. 'Right. That will hopefully take the edge off while we work out how to do some heavy lifting.'

Carly almost didn't want to see what was going on under the branch but somehow, with the help of Michaela, some thick rope and some clever physics Owen came up with, they managed to roll it off Simon's leg, exposing a bone-deep wound across his shin.

As the branch shifted, he moaned and screamed, but now he was eerily quiet and pale. Carly kept a close eye on his blood pressure and breathing while Michaela was sent next door to meet the chopper crew.

Owen pressed two fingers at various points over the man's ankle and foot. Then he did it again, methodically touching and pressing. 'No medial pedal pulses. We need him air-lifted as soon as possible. In the meantime, we need to keep monitoring him and stabilise that fracture.'

The leg was clearly broken, oddly flattened, with deep bleeding cuts and the start of some impressive bruising and swelling. While Owen applied dressings to the gashes, Carly took out her inflatable splint and together they slid it under Simon's leg and inflated it to provide stability and keep him safe until the helicopter arrived.

They were doing another round of vital signs when Simon began to shake uncontrollably.

'Blood pressure is dropping. Ninety over fifty.' Carly watched the electronic machine inflate the cuff around Simon's arm again. 'Pulse is getting faster. One hundred and two.'

Owen put his hand on the man's shoulder. 'Looks like you're in a bit of shock, mate. How about I put in a line and give you some fluids? That should help.'

Carly opened the silver emergency blanket. 'I'll go see if I can find some more blankets in the house.'

'Mind reader.' Owen smiled and took the crinkly blanket, wrapping it around their patient.

She watched as he knelt on the ground, completely unaffected by the thistles and gravel, his focus purely on his patient, and she wondered what it would feel like to have Owen's gaze on her, his focus only on her. Those strong hands around her waist again, the way they'd been on the jet-ski. Pulling her close against his toned body. Holding her.

What the heck? She barely knew the man. Why would she want him to hold her? Why was she thinking about his hands? His body? About the way her body had responded when those hands had spanned her waist?

Because, she realised with a shock, she was attracted to him. Properly attracted, as in intrigued, endeared, interested. Very interested. It felt as if her body was springing to life after years of hibernation, prickling with goosebumps, heating low in her belly. She liked Owen Cooper enough to think about holding him.

Panic radiated through her, making her heart thud against her rib cage. She couldn't. She just couldn't. She couldn't hold anyone, not after everything she'd been through. It was too much of a risk to her heart, which had only just started to heal. She couldn't let herself fall into anything meaningful again. So she forced herself to follow his lead and focus on the needs of the patient.

Mind reader...

'I sincerely hope not,' she quipped back, then dashed to the house to get some more blankets and hopefully find some perspective.

For the second time that day, Owen watched a helicopter rise into the sky.

Carly stood next to him on the jetty, her hand shielding her eyes. The wind whipped strands of her dark hair out of her ponytail, framing her face in wispy waves. Her nose was peeling. Her skin was tanned. She looked vibrant and healthy, like an advert for outdoor exercise. Loose-limbed and free.

She was so different from Miranda, who refused to go anywhere near the sun in case it damaged her skin. And, no, he wouldn't let his bad marriage intrude on his new life...unless it was to facilitate Mason seeing his mother.

Carly bent and riffled through her bag. Thinking she was fishing out the jet-ski keys, he asked her, 'Back to the surgery, then?'

Although, if he was honest, spending a few more moments in this beautiful cove with a beautiful woman was very enticing.

'In a minute or two.' She took out a flask and poured hot liquid into two battered white tin cups with *Rāwhiti Camp* printed on the side in forest-green ink. 'Refreshments first.'

'That's like Mary Poppins's bag.' He pretended to peer inside it. 'Is it bottomless?'

She laughed and followed his eyes to her large rucksack. 'I'm an efficient packer. I teach rucksack packing to the kids before we set off into the bush on our overnight camps. You wouldn't believe the kind of things they like to sneak in there that add so much weight, they complain all the way in and all the way out again.'

'Like what?'

'Books. More food than they could eat for a week—sweets, mainly. All sorts of devices to entertain them. They don't realise they won't have the energy for anything but holding a cup of hot chocolate after I've had them bush whack, build a shelter and then cook their dinner over an open fire.'

'Sounds fun.'

'It is. The kids love it. Some of them have never even seen the sea, can you imagine—living in the city or in a farm in the middle of nowhere and not ever going to the coast? You should see their faces.' She suddenly looked wistful and he remembered she was selling up. Did she want to? Was she being forced to?

He made sure to catch her eye. 'Are you okay, Carly?'

'Sure. I'm fine.' She flashed him a confused look and offered him a cup of hot brown liquid before sitting down at the end of the jetty, her legs hanging over the side. 'Why?'

'You seem…' He wanted to say 'emotional' but knew that wouldn't go down well. 'It's been a stressful afternoon.'

'Simon's leg wound was pretty gruesome, but I've seen worse. But, if you're asking why I need a hot drink and a rest, it's because it's important to stay hydrated, especially when going from one emergency to another. It's easy to forget about eating and drinking in all the hustle and bustle. But even superheroes need a cup of tea every now and then.'

He laughed, sat down next to her, took the cup and sipped the sweet hot tea. Interesting that she'd assumed he was asking her about the accident and not about the sudden change in her demeanour when she'd talked about her job. He wanted to ask so many questions but didn't think it right to pry. He'd hate it if anyone wanted to know all about his business. 'Well, that was certainly an interesting introduction to island life.'

'It's not usually like this.' She turned to look at him at the same moment he turned to look at her. Her eyes sparkled like water in sunlight, like diamonds glittering. 'Don't get too excited, Dr Cooper.'

Interesting choice of words. Especially as the word 'excited' falling from her lips seemed to set off an echoing thrum inside him. But he didn't want to misinterpret anything, and certainly didn't want to imbue the conversation with his wayward thoughts, so he changed direction. 'Look, about the other day…'

'Yes?' She gave a coy sideways glance, eyebrows raised in a question. Her dark eyes played and a smile hovered on her lips.

'Was I really going too fast? Because, if so, I need to get a handle on that boat, especially when I have Mason to look after too. From where I was, it didn't feel too fast.'

There was a long pause, during which Carly sighed and nodded, her smile gone. She slid her foot along the decking. The kind of hedging mannerism that his son did when he didn't want to admit to a wrongdoing. 'Okay, I guess not, if I'm honest. Only, I'm very protective of my little cove and my students.'

'It's good to be safety conscious.'

'Yes.' Her voice was soft. 'But I can be over-the-top protective.'

He wondered why, but that thought dissolved the moment he glanced at his watch. 'Damn, I was supposed to collect Mason ten minutes ago. It's my first pick-up from kindergarten and they'll probably shout me down.'

'No, they won't. They'll be very polite and understanding. Not everyone's as brutally honest as me around here.' She laughed as she bundled the empty cups and flask back into her bag and jumped up. 'Come on, then, jump on.'

He settled behind her on the jet-ski and slid his hands around her waist, feeling her heat against his skin. Her back was ramrod-straight. Sea spray covered the fine hairs on her arms. Her scent—flowers and fresh air—mingled with the salty air and made him want to inhale deeply.

He inched away from her. This was getting ridiculous. He couldn't be attracted to a woman's scent. Or notice the warmth of her skin or her toned legs and, more than anything, the sad smile she had when she thought no one was looking at her.

When they arrived back at the marina, Mia was sitting on the sand with both her own little girl and Mason, building sandcastles. Owen jumped off the jet-ski, helped Carly secure it on the floating dock then ran towards the nurse and his son.

Carly jogged alongside. 'Hey, Mia,' she said with the huge grin she seemed to save for her sister-in-law. 'Bless you for bringing Mason down to meet us. Owen was starting to stress.'

He had been. And it was getting worse. 'Don't

they have a policy for not allowing children out without a named guardian?'

Immediately he'd said it, he wanted to take it back. Mason was safe and sound, playing contentedly in the sand as if he was on holiday. He certainly didn't look as stressed as Owen felt about the delayed pick-up.

The happy smiles on both women's faces fell. Mia was quick to say, 'Jackie would have been happy to keep him until you arrived, but she had to dash off, and there was no one else. I couldn't leave him there all alone.'

'Of course. Yes.' He wrapped his boy in a hug, but Mason brushed him off with, 'Stop it, Daddy. Build a castle.'

Owen turned back to Mia, to find her frowning at him. 'Jackie knows me. We grew up here together. She knows I'm not about to abduct your son. She also left a couple of messages on your phone, but there was no reply from you. We waited as long as we could but, in the end, she had to close up.'

And all the while he'd been having tea and inappropriate thoughts about Carly. He shrugged apologetically. 'No phone service out there.'

'It happens.' Mia nodded. 'We islanders understand. There's a different pace of life here and we help each other out. We have to, because we're isolated, and there are limited services.'

'What the doctor means is thank you.' Carly smiled, pulling Mia's daughter, Harper, onto her lap and blowing a raspberry onto the toddler's belly, making her giggle and squirm.

It was such a happy scene, and he'd ruined it with his own over-protectiveness and city-borne suspicion. 'Yes, yes, I'm so sorry, Mia. I do mean thank you. Thank you very much. I'm sorry if I came across as rude. I'd been worrying about my boy and, being the only parent here, I need to put him first. I'd hate to think of him left there all alone.'

'It's okay. I'm a single parent too. I totally understand. Any time you need me to pick him up, just let me know. It's no hardship at all, and the kids seem to play well together.' But Mia shot Carly a look Owen couldn't read.

'Can I come to your playground again?' Mason asked Carly, completely out of the blue.

'Mason, where are your manners?' Owen reminded his son, then turned back to Carly. 'I'm so sorry. Just say no. It's fine.'

She looked a little uncomfortable at the suggestion, but glanced down at Harper, and her body language immediately softened. 'Yes, of course, Mason, come and play. That would be lovely. I've got a wonderful playground, and I know your place needs sprucing up. I have school children here every Tuesday to Friday, but they go back home on the one o'clock ferry. Why don't you come over one Friday afternoon?'

'Thank you.' Owen knew he didn't deserve such a kindness, but his son did.

'Not a problem.' She looked up at him and grinned, as if she'd won some battle they'd been waging. And…wow… Her eyes shone, and the sun framed her face, and…she really was beautiful. He didn't know what to say, because telling her she was beautiful was the only thing he could think of, and he really, really couldn't do that.

And yet she was still looking at him and he couldn't drag his eyes from her. The world seemed to shrink to just him and her. What was she thinking? Did she get this weird vibe too?

After a beat or two, she nodded and looked at her watch. 'Shoot. Now I really have to dash. These emergencies have derailed my whole day. See you all later.'

Owen watched her jump up from the sand and then trip lightly away, bag in hand. But he refused to turn to watch her go, even though another glimpse of her would be good for…

'So, Dr Cooper. Had a good afternoon with our Carly?'

He turned and saw Mia looking at him with a quizzical expression. He dragged his thoughts away from Carly. 'Eventful, shall we say?'

'Sounds like you handled everything well. A

good team?' She glanced in the direction Carly had headed.

Owen followed her gaze with a little pang in his heart to see no sign of the woman he'd spent the afternoon with. 'We worked well together. It's great that she knows everyone and has the whole routine down pat. It makes my life easier.'

'Underneath all that armour, she's actually lovely.'

'Is she?' He laughed, just to show he was joking, but in truth he wasn't sure where this was going. 'She's definitely capable.'

'Aha. That's what we call it, right?' Mia smiled and raised her eyebrows, as if she was in on some private joke. A joke he hadn't been let in on.

'She handles the jet-ski well and anticipates danger and the right kind of response needed.' And that was as far as he was going to go with this conversation.

'Just…look, Owen…' Mia grimaced. 'Carly's had a hard time. We both have, if I'm going to be honest.'

'I'm sorry to hear that.' Seeing the nurse's eyes fill with tears, he sensed this conversation straying into difficult territory. 'Hey, please. You don't have to tell me anything personal.'

'No doubt you'll hear all about it anyway from one of the locals. It's not a secret.' Carly shook her head and gave Owen a wobbly smile, wiping her cheek with the heel of her hand. 'But I guess it is her story to tell and, if I blab it all, it will sound like gossip, which she'd hate. But...well... she doesn't like to let people close.' Mia swallowed and Owen could see how hard it was for her to be telling him this. 'She has good reasons, Owen. She's been through a lot. Just...be gentle.'

'Are you warning me or...what?' What kind of impression had he given Mia? Or Carly? He'd stuck to being professional, but maybe something had given away his...interest...attraction to Carly? 'Because, I can assure you, we're purely work colleagues.'

Who exactly was he trying to convince here—Mia or himself?

'Sure you are.' Mia jumped up, gathered her bag and the buckets and spades and called to her daughter. 'Harper, come on, missy. Time for tea. See you tomorrow, Owen. Bye, Mason.'

Then she gave him a quick wave and left him there with his son and a whole lot of emotions he couldn't put a name to.

CHAPTER FOUR

IT WASN'T A DATE. Well, it was a *play* date, but that was all. *For Mason*. This outing was just to make his son happy.

So, why Owen felt strangely excited and simultaneously nervous he couldn't say. But his gut tightened just a little when he saw her strolling down the jetty as he tied the rope round the cleat.

In some ways he wished Mia hadn't hinted about Carly's past because he knew it would affect the way he reacted to her. He liked the sparky banter, he was comfortable with that kind of casual interaction and wasn't sure it was a good idea to take things deeper, especially after Miranda and their complicated relationship. He was intrigued by Carly and had to admit to, well, caring about her. If you could care about someone after knowing them for five minutes. But there it was. They had a connection, and he wasn't sure what to do about it.

'Hi, Owen. And Mason!' Carly put out her hand to haul Mason out of the boat onto the jetty.

'Hey, buddy. Seriously? Have you grown since I saw you on Monday?'

'Yes.' The boy nodded solemnly and puffed out his chest.

'His appetite's increased, that's for sure.' Owen climbed out of the boat, carrying a bag of spare clothes and snacks for Mason. 'He's eating me out of house and home.'

'All this fresh air does them a world of good.' Her hair was loose today, soft titian waves framing her face and skimming her shoulders. Her skin glowed. She was wearing a teal-blue gypsy-style top with beads sewn around the V-neck, a long tiered white skirt, beaded sandals and, unexpectedly, bright red nail varnish on her toe nails. Which made him curious. It was so feminine and fun. There were clearly other sides to Carly's personality than supremely efficient first responder and over-all superhero.

She looked like something from a magazine advertising healthy living as she nodded at him and smiled. 'So, how was the rest of your first week on Rāwhiti?'

'Not as exciting as the first day. Luckily, we've been quiet, because it's only been Mia and myself, what with Anahera being with her family. But now I'm proficient in answering the phones and making appointments and attending to any queries as well as seeing patients.'

Her eyebrows rose as she grinned. 'You have to be a Jack of all trades here. I'm glad you've managed.'

'Oh, it's nothing compared to the eighteen-thousand-patient practice I had before. The mornings have been calm, with no call-outs and need for babysitters in the evenings, which I'm grateful for. We needed to get into a proper routine, and being AWOL for pick-up was not a good start.'

'Seriously, no one minds if you turn up late, or even early. We're all very flexible here. Right, come on, Mason! The playground's been waiting all afternoon to see you.' She jogged along the jetty towards the little playground area with Mason skipping by her side, giggling with excitement.

Owen's chest contracted as he watched the way his son looked up at her with abject adoration.

Don't get too close, boy. She's leaving.

Was this a mistake? Should he have insisted they stay away? The poor kid had already been abandoned by his mother. Was Owen setting him up for more heartbreak? Panic rattled through him but he breathed it out. They were here now. He'd let him play today and then gently discourage him from coming back.

By the time he got to the playground, Mason had skipped off to climb the ladder at the back of the slide, leaving Owen and Carly alone. They stood under the shade of a flowering *pohutukawa* tree, its fallen red stamens carpeting the ground like a scarlet blanket. Native flax and clivia bordered the sides of the little play area that gave onto a large grassy area leading down to the shoreline.

'Watch me, Daddy!' Mason sat at the top of the slide then inched forward and down. 'Whee!'

Seeing the happiness on his son's face convinced him that this had been a good idea. He'd just have to wean him off the camp and the camp owner. Although, she'd be gone soon enough. Which was enough of a reminder that he could admire the woman from a distance, but that was all it could ever be for him.

She smiled up at him. 'So, how's the old Nelson place treating you?'

'Nelson place? Where's that?' Had he missed something?

'The previous owner of your house was called Horatio, so his nickname had to be Nelson, right? When he died last year, he bequeathed the house to the Rāwhiti Island Community Trust and we voted on it being used as the doctor's house as a lure to bring a medic over here. But I realise it needs work.'

He laughed as he thought about his feathered friend alarm clock and the holes in the walls that needed blocking. 'It needs bowling, to be honest. I'm waiting on an order from the hardware store over in Auckland, but I'm not entirely sure when it'll arrive.'

'These things take time. I've got some old bits of timber out the back if you need them.' She pointed over to the little cottage on the edge of the shore. 'Happy for you to take a look. Once this place is sold, I'll have to get rid of everything like that anyway, so you might as well have it.'

She's leaving. She's leaving.

'Great. Thanks. I'll take a look. I could drive over and collect what doesn't fit in my boat.'

'I don't think you'll fit much in that.' She laughed, her brown eyes shining. 'I can get the ferry to bring the big stuff round, don't worry.'

'They do that?'

She gave him a questioning look. 'Has no one explained that to you? We charter barges to bring big items in, but the ferry brings small things over for us, and there's the mail run boat three times a week. Which means I get to do as much online shopping as anyone in the city.'

'I bet you don't do as much as my wife does. In fact, I doubt anyone shops as much as Miranda.'

'Wife?' Carly blinked, and her demeanour changed from soft and light to something more guarded. He immediately regretted bringing his past into the conversation.

'*Ex*-wife.'

'Mason's mum? Where is she?'

'In the States. She's an actress, and that's the best place to be for her career.'

An eyebrow rose, and with it all the judgement he'd felt from everyone he explained their situation to. 'She had a job opportunity she couldn't turn down,' he quickly explained.

'And you couldn't go with her? She couldn't take her son?' Carly looked over at Mason, her expression one of affection mixed with concern. 'He must miss her.'

'Let's just say there wasn't an invitation for me and my boy.'

She looked back at Owen and frowned. 'I see.'

'Actually, I'm not sure you do.'

She held up her hand and shook her head. 'Hey, it's none of my business—'

'No, but it makes her sound callous, and she isn't, just...' He searched for the right word to describe Miranda without casting too dark a light on his ex. 'Self-absorbed and career-focused. She never wanted kids, and I knew that going into the marriage. When she accidentally fell pregnant, I hoped her attitude might change, but it didn't. She gave it a go, for my sake really, I think, although I didn't pressurise her either way. But she found family life suffocating and difficult. She stuck it out for just over three years and, believe me, I tried hard to be the husband and father we needed me to be—to be present and give them what they both needed—but I also had to work to pay the bills and was growing the business too. So I spent the week working all hours at the practice and then tried to make up for it at weekends.'

Why was he telling her all this?

Carly blew out a breath. 'Sounds like a lot of pressure.'

'Yes, and Miranda couldn't cope. She genuinely tried. But it wasn't the life she wanted. And, sadly, we weren't the people she wanted around her in Los Angeles.'

She gave a curious frown. 'I meant a lot of pressure for you, Owen.'

He looked over at his son, screaming with pleasure as he slid down the slide again. 'Mason's no pressure at all, apart from fuelling my determination to be two parents instead of one. In that, I can honestly say, I'm failing. At least, I was. It became very clear very quickly that I couldn't work full-time and only see him asleep. Which I did for a few months after Miranda left, because I was trying to maintain Mason's routine with the help of a nanny, but he suffered. We both did. I barely saw him, and when we did spend time together it was like two strangers not knowing how to react or reconnect. So I took this job, which is half the hours I was working in the city. And now I get to be a rubbish parent for more hours each day.' He huffed at the irony. 'Lucky kid.'

'You're not a rubbish parent. I've seen you in action, and I've seen you go all growly protective over him.'

'Not my finest moment.' He grimaced, wishing she'd forgotten about his *faux pas* on the beach with Mia.

'Look, you've seen me growly protective over kids that aren't even mine. I get it.' There was a pause, then her tone turned tentative. 'How can you not be angry at her for leaving?'

'I was. I am. I mean, look at him—how could you not want to be here and see him grow? But I knew she didn't want kids. I can't blame her for being the person I always knew she was. And she does try to stay in touch, although time zones and filming schedules don't always work in our favour.'

Carly's eyes widened and she smiled. 'You're a better person than me, Owen Cooper. I'd be furious.'

'I'm angry that she left Mason, of course, because he's too young to understand her reasons, and he's acted out and grieved. He misses her.'

The boy in question was now chasing a weka across the grass. Carly laughed as she watched him. 'He's a good kid.'

'He is. Although not quite mature enough to

realise that no weka is ever going to let him catch them. They're fast.'

'They also eat the baby ducklings and steal the kids' food if they're not watching out.' She started to follow Mason. 'They're a pain. Funny, but a pain.'

'I know. I have one as an alarm clock.' He fell into step with her, but she came to a halt and turned to him.

'A what?'

He laughed, although he'd stopped thinking it was funny by Wednesday, the fifth morning he'd been woken by the tapping. 'There's a hole in the kitchen wall and a very clever weka manages to squeeze through it and into the house. I've tried to cover it over with what bits of wood I can find and a makeshift hammer—aka my shoe heel—and some nails I found in an old, dusty jam jar in the shed, and I've stuffed the hole with news-paper, but the damned bird always manages to work its way in.'

'You definitely need my timber and tools. I can come and help, if you like. It's no trouble. I like getting my hands dirty. I built the barbe-cue area last year and it hasn't fallen down...yet.' She pointed over to the very impressive barbecue area on a flat concrete standing, with a wooden arbour overhead.

'Looks great. You built that?'

'What? Don't you think a woman could build something like that?' She growled but her eyes sparked humour. Her hands hit her waist. It was a gauntlet.

He held up his palms in surrender. 'Whoa. No assumptions here. I'm just impressed that anyone who isn't a qualified builder could make that.' The struts of the arbour were interlaced and there was a trellis at the back with a mandevilla plant climbing up it. 'It looks like a professional job.'

'I like to think so.' She pursed her lips. 'It's just me here. I can't wait around for someone to help me do stuff. I just have to get stuck in.'

'If you can do that, then I'll definitely take you up on the offer.'

She grinned. 'Excellent. I'll drop some stuff round tomorrow and we'll take it from there.'

'Great.' He imagined her, all grubby in her short shorts, and his body prickled in response. Every cell felt awake and alive and tugged towards her. And, inconveniently, he realised it wasn't just a physical attraction. He wanted to find out more about her. To uncover the story Mia had hinted at. To uncover Carly Edwards.

Whoa. He hadn't expected to feel anything like this again. Not for a long time, anyway. But then, he hadn't expected meeting the whirlwind that was this woman. His focus had to be on Mason. He should have been building barriers, not thinking of her building barbecues and getting all dirty...

In an effort to douse the ripple of need thrumming through him he asked, 'Give us a tour of the camp?'

She glanced at the row of buildings behind them. 'Oh, yes. Of course. Hey, Mason, come and see what else we've got around here.'

Camp Rāwhiti was a fully equipped educational facility with a huge kitchen and dining room, bunk rooms, bathroom facilities, the barbecue area Carly had built, a laundry and drying room. Deeper into the bush was a ropes course designed to build confidence, strength and endurance, evidence of bivouac-building by previous students and, at the top of a steep incline, an observatory for viewing the stars. On the shore side was a quaint white cottage where Carly lived, neat and pristine with a plentiful vegetable garden bursting with produce. Next to that was the boat shed.

'What's in there?' Mason pointed to the shed.

Carly rolled back the door to show him. 'We've got paddle boards, little optimist sailing boats and kayaks.'

Mason frowned as he peered in. 'What's a kayak?'

Owen cringed. The boy had grown up in Auckland, the self-proclaimed City of Sails, but they'd barely been to the beach, never mind on the water. It had been busy enough doing the chores every weekend, setting them up with food for the week and doing the laundry. He'd barely had the energy, never mind the time, to do day trips.

His eyes met Carly's and he wanted to tell her he wasn't a bad parent, just a busy one, but she just smiled. 'It's like a little boat that you sit right in and paddle out on the water. It's great fun. We've had dolphins and whales visit us in this bay and they like to show off to the kayakers.'

'Can I try kayak, Daddy? With Carly too?'

Uh-uh. Mason was wheedling his way into this woman's life. He ruffled the boy's hair. 'Not today, buddy. Carly's busy.'

She beamed at the boy. 'Actually, it's getting a bit late, and it takes a lot of time to paddle out and back. How about next Friday after kindy? We'll go out straight away.'

Mason nodded, his big, dark eyes pleading and irresistible. 'Yes, please.'

'Good. Mr Mason, do we have a date?' She put her hand out to shake.

Mason turned and looked up at Owen, his eyes wide, his little body trembling with excitement. 'Kayak, Daddy! Kayak! Kayak!'

Oh, God. What was he doing letting Mason spend more time here? But seeing him so excited made Owen's heart squeeze. He couldn't remember the last time Mason had shown such enthusiasm for something. What they both needed was distance from Carly, not more time with her. On the other hand, he wanted to protect his son from more heartache, but surely learning to kayak would be a great life skill?

They were both looking at him expectantly. He reluctantly nodded at his son. 'Shake Carly's hand like a gentleman. Firm, but not tight. Seal the deal.'

After they made their solemn agreement, Owen turned towards the playground, but Carly said from behind him, 'Right. You two head over to the outside tables and I'll bring the picnic over.'

'Picnic? You didn't have to cook anything.'

She shrugged it off with a smile. 'It's a lovely evening, and I know kids like to eat early. It's not much, but I'm sure it'll fill him up.'

How could he refuse? 'Can I help?'

'No, it's all ready. You stay and watch him. I won't be long.'

So, even though he'd have much preferred to watch her languidly stride across the grass, he took his son to the swings and pushed him.

'Higher and higher, Daddy!'

Afterwards they sat on a wooden picnic table and ate home-made sausage rolls, which Mason exclaimed were the best he'd ever had, with salad and chopped vegetables, and fresh home-grown strawberries for dessert, and chatted about life on the island and Mason's week in kindy.

Which, it transpired, had been lots of fun and, even though Mason hadn't really opened up to his father, he was very chatty with Carly now. Apparently, his son had made a collage, played with bricks, been to the beach on an outing and done some art. Which was all news to Owen, because the most he ever got out of his son at pickup time was, 'Good, thanks,' in answer to, 'How was your day?'

When would that change?

When Mason went back for a final play on the playground, Carly wandered over and sat on a nearby wooden bench, keeping her eye on the boy.

Owen slid in next to her, out of touching distance, but next to her.

A gold plaque on the back of the bench caught his eyes.

In loving memory of Wendy, Malcolm and Rafferty Edwards
They loved this place
Sit a while and remember all the good things
They'd want you to be as happy here as they were

Edwards. Carly's surname. Who were these people?

He sensed her watching him so he turned his gaze to the kitchen block behind them. 'This is a big place. How many kids do you have at a time?'

'Depends on the school. We can take up to a hundred.'

'I can't believe you run the place by yourself. Does Mia work here as well as being a nurse?'

'She helps with the admin, that's all. She doesn't have time for anything else. I have a couple of employees who help me out when things get busy. But mainly it's just me, the teachers from the school and the parent helpers.'

'How do you manage it all?'

'It's a well-oiled machine. Most of the schools have been using this place for years, they know how it all works. They bring all their own food and bedding, and the parent helpers cook and are allocated to small groups of students. The kids clean up. It's a lot of fun for them all.'

'It sounds like it. So, did you buy it?'

'God, no. I couldn't afford to buy a property like this, it's worth millions.' Her forehead crinkled with a frown. 'Mia and I inherited half each when her parents died.'

'Okay.' Which didn't explain much to him.

But her hands tightened into fists on her lap. She pressed her lips together, as if trying to hold in a scream or a cry, then eventually said, 'Along with my husband. They all died together. In an accident.'

Wendy and Malcolm and Rafferty. The corners of the gold plaque jutted into his back. He sat forward, wanting to cover her hand with his. Wanting to pull her close and just hold her, anything to wipe away the haunted grief on her face, to take away some of the pain she must have been carrying.

He turned to face her properly. 'Oh, Carly. I'm so sorry. But please, you don't have to go over it all. You don't have to tell me.'

She shook her head, her eyes filled with tears. 'You'll hear about it soon enough. In fact, I'm surprised you don't know already. I thought Mia might have told you. They were out on the boat. A freak wave, we think, during a storm. You know what it's like here, we have four seasons in one day. It's beautiful in the morning and by lunchtime there's a deluge. It's predictably unpredictable. All we know is that one day the three of them went out on the water and never came back. Their boat was eventually found in pieces at the far end of the island. And Malcolm's—Mia and Raff's dad—body washed up on Kawau island, a few miles west of here. No one else was ever found.'

He didn't know what to say. Nothing could make this better. 'I'm so sorry, Carly.'

She shrugged, the corner of her mouth turning into a sort of resigned half-smile. 'It's okay.'

'No, it's not. It's tragic. It's awful. No wonder you're so concerned about safety on the water.'

'I always was, because it's stupid not to be, but I'm pretty intense about it now. I'm sorry I blasted you on your first day here. You must have thought I was horrible.'

'Scary.' He wiggled his eyebrows.

She laughed. 'Good. It means you took notice.'

'Oh, I noticed all right.' He probably shouldn't have said that—actually, he *definitely* shouldn't have said it—but it was too late.

She looked up at him, surprise softening her features. But she didn't look shocked, disgusted or angry. Her smile grew sad, yet hopeful. 'Yes. Me too.'

Something inside him felt as if it was cracking open, as if they'd made a breakthrough. As if this moment was significant. He didn't know why or how, just that it meant something. Carly Edwards was important and special.

And yet how could she be? She was leaving, he was staying and they were both protecting their hearts. And he was protecting Mason's too.

But they were talking about her losses and he wasn't going to detract from that. 'Tell me about him. About Rafferty?' He guessed that was her husband.

The smile she gave him now was filled with gratitude and he wondered if she'd been wanting to talk about this but hadn't known how to start.

'I met him on a holiday in Nepal. We were both into the same things: the outdoors, fitness, nature. We just clicked immediately and, even though I'd planned to see much more of the world on my gap year, it was his last stop before heading home. But it just felt natural and right for me to come with him. I met his family and, well, you know Mia, they're so loving and inclusive, and I felt as if I'd finally found my "for ever" place.'

His gut knotted into a tight ball. Sitting on this bench with the plaque rubbing against his back, he was well aware the ending wasn't happy. 'And then…?'

'We got married and were planning to live and work here and bring up our family, like his parents had. When he died, I didn't have anywhere else to go, so I stayed.'

'How so? No family? You're English, right?'

'Yes. But no family.' At his frown, she rushed on. 'Apart from Mia and Harper. But now I think it's time to spread my wings, see what I want to do with the rest of my life. They would hate that I was so torn up over it and they'd encourage me to find out who I am again. Me. Not a wife. Not a daughter-in-law.'

A beautiful, competent, smart woman who deserved the very best in life. 'You have plans?'

'Not really. Probably back to Nepal to pick up where I left off and to pay a sort of homage to Raff. Where it all started, you know?'

She had obviously adored her husband. 'Sounds like a great starting point. And then you can have an adventure.'

'Exactly. I've been here for five years, having been absorbed into this place without really thinking everything through. I just need some headspace away from here to work out what I want and who I am.' She sat up straighter and her eyes sparkled.

He had to admit that his admiration for her grew deeper. 'What if you decided you wanted to come back here? Can't you find temporary managers?'

'I've tried, believe me. But it takes a special kind of person to run this place and we just haven't found the right fit. So we made the decision to sell it.' She inhaled deeply and he could see she was torn by the decision. It would be hard, giving up this connection with the man she'd loved.

'What does Mia think about you wanting to sell up?'

At the mention of her sister-in-law's name, she beamed. 'She's sad, of course, because she grew up at the camp, but she's realistic enough to know she can't expect me to keep it going. She always wanted to be a nurse, so running this place has never been on her agenda. And now she has little Harper too, she said she can use the cash from the sale as a nest egg and it'll give her options in the future.'

Here was an opportunity to clear another question up. 'I don't mean to be nosy, but she said she was a single parent too…?'

'Oh, she's a secretive one, is our Mia. Even I don't know who Harper's dad is. Mia's been very tight-lipped on that, all through the pregnancy and the last eighteen months since the birth. She's never said a word about him.'

'Oh, I do like a mystery.'

Carly laughed. 'Trust me, if she hasn't told me, she's not going to tell you.'

'You never know. I might have special charms.'

'I think you probably do.' Laughing, she looked up at him and gave him a very pretty smile. The air around them seemed to still. She was caught in a sunbeam of light, her hair firing red and gold, her eyes a soulful brown. He didn't think he'd ever seen anyone look more beautiful. For a moment he was transfixed and couldn't take his eyes off her.

He held her gaze for just long enough to know she'd meant it exactly the way he'd thought she had and it was both a shock and a thrill to realise she might have the same weird feelings he had.

He thought about the connotations of her words. God knew what was going on inside her head, but she was looking at him with the same expression he felt. That this was…something.

His gaze slid from her eyes to her mouth. Her lips were blush-pink, full and lush. Perfect for kissing.

What would she taste like? Fresh strawberries?

She'd just told him about her tragic past and he wanted to comfort her, but more too. He shouldn't think about kissing her. But, damn, he really wanted to.

And still she was looking at him, her gaze heated and misted, as if she was wondering how he would taste. Before he knew what he was doing, he slid his hand over hers.

She blinked but didn't pull her hand away.

Thoughts crowded his head. *Too fast. Too soon. Too stupid. Too rash. Too beautiful. Too…everything.*

He tugged his fingers from hers and jumped back as reality seeped into his muddled brain. What the actual hell was he doing? He stood and shoved his hands into his pockets. 'Shoot. I'm sorry. I don't know what just happened.'

She shook her head, eyes startled, as if working through the ramifications too. 'It's…okay.'

'No, it isn't.' For so many reasons—not least because they were so close to where Mason was playing. How would he explain that to a four-year-old?

His son was still chattering away on the far side of the slide. Owen walked across the playground, trying to control his rattling heart and raging libido. 'Mason? Are you done? It's time to go.'

CHAPTER FIVE

WHY WAS SHE offering to help him? Why was she allowing herself to fall deeper and deeper under this little family of two's spell? She had no business getting to know them more. Owen was a good man, underneath the gruffness. Mason was a cutie who just needed coaxing out of his shell.

But she was not the one to do the coaxing. She was heading off on an adventure.

And now...? Well, now she was just being neighbourly, the way she'd helped Horatio towards the end, and the way she baked cupcakes for Mia and Harper. Or the way she... Carly hit the steering wheel of her old truck. 'Who am I trying to kid?'

She wasn't being neighbourly—she was getting involved. She'd wanted to kiss him last night, so badly. Only the thought of Mason catching them had stopped her.

But what if the boy hadn't been there? Would she have kissed him?

She would have. Unlike other men she'd met

since Raff's death, and the few boyfriends before she'd met her husband, Owen seemed to get her. There was an unspoken understanding. Something deepening. She couldn't explain it. The only other person she'd ever felt such a connection with had been her husband.

Was that a bad sign?

Truth was, it was all a bad sign, given that she was leaving.

The driveway to the old Nelson one-storey cottage was winding and gravelled and by the time she arrived she felt as if she was covered in a sheen of dust. As she stepped out of her truck, Mason ran out of the door. 'Carly! Carly!'

Her heart tripped at the grinning boy. 'Hey, Mason. How's it going?'

'Good.' He ran back to the front door. 'Daddy! Carly's here.'

'Great. Thanks, Mason. Now, go finish your call.' Owen stepped out of the front door and her heart didn't just trip, it stumbled. He was dressed in a faded grey T-shirt and battered jeans. His hair looked damp, as if it had just been washed, and it curled cutely up at the edges. His city skin was sun-kissed now, his toned arms tanned. He was gorgeous as he smiled. 'Hey, Carly. How's it going?'

Her mouth was dry. Words were lost somewhere in the mix of attraction and heat, but she managed a husky, 'Great, thanks. I've brought some wood and tools over. Thought we could have a look at fixing the weka version of a cat flap.'

His smile broadened. 'I never thought of it like that.'

She looked past him for Mason, who'd disappeared back inside. There was safety in having the child around. There'd be no hand-holding in front of Owen's son. 'Does Mason want to help too?'

Owen shook his head. 'He's on a call with his mum.'

'Oh.' Her stomach knotted. Why, she didn't know. It was none of her business. 'Bad timing?'

'No, it's fine. They're just finishing up.' He grimaced. 'They don't need me around for that.'

Silly woman, giving him up. 'Well, anyway. I'll just drop this stuff and head back home.'

'Let me get it.' He strode across to the truck's open flatbed tray and reached into it for the planks of wood. As he stretched, the hem of his T-shirt lifted, giving her a bird's eye view of rippling abs.

Stop looking. Her mouth wasn't just watering, it was positively drooling now. She dragged her gaze back to the planks of wood and gave herself a good talking to. *Just being neighbourly. You're leaving.*

Grabbing her tool bag, she followed him back to the house. 'Right. Where's the hole the weka gets through?'

He leaned the planks against the wall, then crouched down, brushed some low bushes away from the side of the house and showed her the ragged weka-sized hole. 'Don't know if it's wear and tear, or whether it's been hit by something.'

She crouched down next to him and leaned forward to examine the hole at the same time he did. He must have sensed they were going to touch the broken wood at the same time she did, because he jerked away. As they both reeled backwards, she caught a hint of his scent: shampoo and soap and something distinctly masculine that made her insides buzz with need.

This was getting ridiculous. How could the way a man smelt make her tummy tumble?

She focused on the rip in the side of the house. 'It looks like a hit to me. Nelson had Parkinson's and couldn't manage at all without help at the end. I wouldn't be surprised if he reversed his car into it or something at some point, and possibly didn't even notice. With the bushes growing so tall here, we didn't notice either when we came to stock the place up for you. You want me to fix it for you?'

'Thanks, Carly.' Owen gave her a savvy smile

and shook his head. 'I know I'm a city slicker, but I can manage this.'

'Go right ahead.' She stood up and crossed her arms, happy to watch him work. But she'd only said she'd drop the things off, not leer at his muscles. 'Oh. Right. Yes. I'll get going—'

'Carly!'

She turned to see Mason running towards her, arms outstretched as he chased a weka. 'Carly, this is my friend.'

'Also known as my alarm clock.' Owen straightened and laughed as he watched his son. God, they were both irresistible. 'Although, there are a few around here, and I can't tell them apart. So it could be a different bird each time.'

'No, Daddy. This one is my friend. He's got sticky-up feathers on his head.' Mason stopped chasing and came over to her. 'His name is Wallace. Like *Wallace and Gromit*.'

Carly laughed. 'I love those films.'

'Me too.'

'*The Wrong Trousers* is the funniest thing I've ever seen.' She watched the weka escape across the dusty path towards the undergrowth and laughed to herself. She was going to have to have a word with Owen about little Wallace.

Owen hammered the last nail into a piece of timber covering the hole. 'I defy the little blighter to get through that. Right. Thirsty work. You want a glass of something cold?'

'Err, I think I should go.'

'Okay. But don't blame me if you miss out on the best lemonade this side of the island.' His eyebrows rose, as if in a dare.

'Oh? Fighting talk. You've obviously never tried mine.' And she could never turn down a dare, so she followed man and boy into the kitchen. The cupboards and floor had been scrubbed and the place looked spotless—tired and old, but spotless. 'Wow. This looks a lot cleaner than when Nelson lived here.'

'We try our best, don't we, Mason? Looks like Carly's impressed with our work, buddy.' He held up his hand and his son gave him a high-five. 'Good job, son.'

Owen's mini-me looked up at him as if he was the sun, moon and stars all rolled into one. 'Good job, Dad!'

Carly's chest heated. She'd never had a connection with a blood relative, so didn't know how it felt to be praised by a parent, but she understood the look in Mason's eyes. Despite their difficult times, she knew that these two would grow closer and closer. It would have been nice to watch it all unfold.

Owen washed his hands in the big white butler's sink, poured them all a glass of lemonade and they clinked their glasses together, as if they were a team. She had to admit, 'This is really good lemonade.'

The corners of Owen's mouth turned up into a beautiful smile. Praise looked good on him. 'The trick is to use the peel too, not just the juice.'

'I'll give it a go.' The scent of tomatoes and garlic filled the air. She turned to the old cooker and saw a pan bubbling with sauce. 'And, hmm… something smells good.'

'We having 'getti Bolo-nose. I stirred it.' Mason's chest puffed out. 'You want some?'

'Spaghetti Bolognaise,' Owen clarified. 'And, trust me, you might like my lemonade, but you don't want to eat my cooking.'

This was the kind of family she craved, like the one she'd lost. She craved real food, a real connection. A willingness to do better, be better. But she had too many reasons not to stay. 'No, I'm okay. I mean… I'm not saying I don't want to eat your food. I just…should probably go.'

Owen's eyebrows peaked, as if he was rethinking his earlier statement. 'There's plenty. It's fine, really. It won't poison you.'

The heat in her chest thickened into an ache. Was she trying to run away because she was scared of caring about these people? Rafferty would have laughed at her. So would his mother, who was a stickler for manners and gratitude.

Feeding people is a sign of respect and friendship here on the island. We don't have much but, what we do have, we share.

So what kind of an example would she be if she turned them down? Plus, she hadn't got round to preparing her own dinner today, and it did smell delicious. 'Okay. Thank you. But I can't stay late, I have a ton of things to do. I've got a viewer coming to see the camp tomorrow.'

'A buyer?'

'Prospective.' She held up her crossed fingers. 'Wish me luck.'

'So it's happening.' He smiled, but there was something else else there too. She tried not to read too much into it. Was it…sadness? Regret? And she noticed that he didn't wish her luck, as she'd asked.

She felt like butterflies were fluttering in her stomach when she thought about selling up. Kind of the way she felt every time she looked at Owen. And there it was: confusion, excitement, apprehension and fear, all mixed up. 'It might be. This is the third viewer we've had come to look the place over, but the estate agent says this one is super-keen.'

'How do you feel?'

'Sad about leaving, but excited too.'

'Yeah. I know that feeling. I had it when we got on the ferry with our suitcases to come here.

Leaving what we knew for something completely new. Wish I'd had the foresight to bring some paint and tools, though.' He looked round the room and grimaced. 'Anyway, this is ready. Mason, can you please set the table?'

They sat round the wooden kitchen table and ate the rustic dinner. Conversation was easy, especially with Mason there too, entertaining them by pulling silly faces, which they all joined in with. It was roundly agreed that Carly could pull the funniest one.

Then, after clearing up, Owen scraped back his chair. 'It's a clear night. Let's go outside and light the fire pit.'

Even though it was way past time for her to leave, Carly just couldn't bring herself to. *Ten more minutes.* 'Do you have marshmallows? We could cook them on sticks.'

'Strangely, I do. There were a few things in the cupboards when we arrived. Coffee, tea—that kind of stuff—and some marshmallows.'

'That was my idea.' She grinned. 'We thought you'd need some basics to help settle in.'

'Marshmallows are basics?' He reached into the cupboard and brought out a bright pink packet.

'For fire pits, yes. Come on, Mason. Let's go find some sticks for the marshmallows…'

* * *

After eating melted, delicious gooeyness, Mason fell asleep on his dad's knee, head lolling over to the side. Owen hauled the boy and himself to standing and spoke quietly. 'I'll just pop him into bed.'

She forced herself to grab the opportunity to leave. 'I'll get going, then.'

But Owen frowned. 'Really? It won't take long. To be honest, I could do with some adult company after spending all day talking with a four-year-old. I mean, I love him to bits, but there's only so much kiddie talk I can take.' He batted his eyelashes. 'Please? Ten minutes?'

She sighed. Did the man know just how gorgeous he was, and how hard it was for her to keep her distance? One little request and she was putty in his hands. 'Okay. Ten minutes. I'll make some hot chocolate while you put him to bed.'

'You certainly know about home comforts.'

She followed him back into the house, whispering, 'I run a school camp, Owen. I know what kids need to help them get over homesickness. And, funnily enough, adults love the comfort too.'

He was back in no time and sat down next to her in front of the fire pit on a rickety wooden chair. The sun was setting and dark orange and red filled the sky, illuminated by flashes of sparks rising from the fire. When Owen smiled, it felt as if the flames flickering between them were in her belly.

He took the cup of hot chocolate and sipped. 'Now, that is delicious. Thanks for all the help, Carly. I really appreciate it.'

'Just being neighbourly.' She forced herself to shrug nonchalantly, even though she felt anything but.

He raised his eyebrows. They both knew there was a lot more to it than that. 'Well, thanks anyway.'

A bird's cry disturbed the silence and she remembered why she'd been smiling earlier on. 'Oh. Yes. Owen, I'm sorry to have to tell you this, but Wallace is actually Wilma.'

'Sorry?'

'He's not a boy weka. He's a girl.' She couldn't help but laugh at the distraught look on his face as her words sank in.

'Ah.' He guffawed. 'Call myself a doctor? I should know the difference.'

'I would hope you do.'

'Believe me, I do when it matters.'

She almost choked on her drink. The thought of the good doctor knowing exactly how to act when it mattered made her hot all over. She managed a coughed-out, 'Thank God for that.'

When she glanced over at him, she realised he

was watching her, his eyes alight as he laughed too. What was he thinking? That this was too cosy? Too sweet? Too hot?

Or that she was truly just a neighbour?

He shrugged. 'Oh well, Mason will never know if I don't tell him.'

'Owen Cooper, are you going to lie to your son?' She laughed some more, feeling more relaxed than she had for a very long time.

'Hey, I already do. Who's the Tooth Fairy and Father Christmas? The Easter Bunny? None of them exist. It's all make-believe.'

'I guess. He's a lucky kid. I don't remember having those kinds of fairy-tales when I was growing up.'

He shuffled closer and frowned as his gaze searched her face. 'Really? No Father Christmas? No Easter Bunny?'

'They're not so big on the bunny in England. Or maybe they are these days, but not when I was growing up. I was lucky if there was a present under the Christmas tree with my name on it. And I'm not saying that for you to feel sorry for me. It's just what it was.'

'Why? Didn't your family believe in Christmas? Or was it something else…?' The fun in his eyes died and they turned sad—for her, even though he had no idea what her story was.

His innate compassion reverberated through

her and she felt embarrassed that she'd snapped at him at their first meeting, assuming the worst. But that kind of suspicion had been programmed into her from an early age.

'I was taken away from my mum when I was eight months old and placed in foster care. Then spent many years being shunted from foster home to foster home, being moved on for a host of different reasons. The family I'd been placed with were moving, or pregnant with their first child and didn't have space for me, or a divorce... It never seemed fair to me that I was the one who had to go. But, well, there it was. So, if I was with a good family there could be a present, but I learnt not to expect anything in case I was taken away.'

'God, Carly, that's awful.' He really did look as if he meant it too.

'It is what it is. The children's home did the present thing, but we all knew it was the staff who bought them. There was always some older kid willing to tell you the truth about where the presents came from, to show you they were so much more clever and so much older.

'One year, I was in a foster home right up until the week before Christmas. There was a present under the tree with my name on and I was so excited about opening it. Then stuff happened and I was uplifted and moved on.' She could still remember the wrapping paper design after all these years. The reindeer with the bright red nose and the jolly Santa. 'So, I'd never really known what it meant to be fully part of a loving family, where you were loved unconditionally, until I came here and met the Edwards family.'

Here she was telling him things she'd never told anyone and yet it felt natural to confide in him. Was it because he was a doctor and he knew about confidentiality? That she trusted him to keep her secrets? Or was it because he was a genuinely good guy?

She trusted him…or was beginning to. That was a revelation, especially after such a short time knowing him.

He drained his cup and placed it on the ground. 'And your birth mum?'

'I don't know much about my birth parents. I have a birth certificate with my mum's name on it and just an empty space where my dad's name should have been. My mother was very young, apparently. Clearly, she couldn't cope with having a baby. Maybe I was a mistake she didn't want.'

It occurred to her that that was exactly what Mason was to his own mother. And it made her like Owen even more that he was so determined to care for his son.

'You are absolutely not a mistake.' He slid his hand over hers and gripped it, all the while his gaze fixed on hers. She could see the flash of censure in his eyes at her words and felt the power of it flicker through her. He wanted her to believe in herself. She liked very much that he was so passionate about it—liked it too much. Liked *him* too much.

A warning thud in her heart almost made her slip her hand out from under his, but it felt right to be talking about her life with someone who wanted to listen, who *saw* her, wanted to hold her hand and give her comfort. It had been so long since she'd felt this close to anyone.

She had to be honest and admit she was lonely here…even with the hundreds of kids who came through every week, and with her sister-in-law down the road and the lovely community on the island. Everyone had been so supportive since the accident, but she was lonely and pining for physical contact, for affection and caring. And to give all that too. But, as always, she put on a brave face. 'Well, my inauspicious beginnings don't matter, really. Here I am. Doing okay.'

'Better than okay. You're amazing, if a little scary.' Smiling, he squeezed her hand. 'You don't want to find her, your mum?'

'No. I don't want to look back any more. I'm so tired of living in the past—although I don't ever want to forget Raff and his parents,' she added hurriedly, as if they were all looking down on her and listening. Maybe they were. And, *if* they were, they'd know how hard she'd hurt and for how long. How much she still missed them. Every day.

Owen smiled gently. 'Of course not.'

'But I'm all about looking forward now.'

'Ah. Your adventure.' The light in his eyes dimmed a little, or maybe it was just the flames in front of them dying down. She couldn't tell.

'My adventure.' And there it was. The reminder of why she shouldn't be sitting so close to him. She tugged her hand away and wedged it under her thigh in case it had any ideas about fitting itself back into his hand again. 'Anyway. What about you?'

'Boring, really.' A shoulder rose and then fell. 'My parents split up when I was eight and I lived with my dad.'

'Unusual.'

He looked over to the house where his sleeping son was. 'Not so much, it seems.'

Indeed. 'What happened to your mum?'

'They split up because she had an affair with someone she worked with and then moved in with the guy. Dad said he wanted me to stay in the family home, and she agreed. So, my dad brought me up…after a fashion. Let's just say he didn't read the rule book on parenting, so I'm learning a whole lot of new things. Like the importance of routine and boundaries. It's been a steep learning curve.'

Which explained why he'd been so irritated to have missed kindy pick-up the other day. He was just trying to get it right. 'Do you see much of your mum?'

'Not really. She has another life and another family now. She moved to Christchurch for her new man's job. We lived in Auckland, so I saw her in the holidays. Sometimes.'

That last word was tinged with sadness. 'Not often?'

'It got difficult. We'd plan things and then she'd cancel. My dad didn't handle it well and there were arguments. That was worse than her not showing up.'

'That's why you're keen to keep Mason's mum in the picture.'

'It's important to me that he stays in contact with her. I really didn't want it to be like this, but what can you do?' He shrugged, palms up, as if he was okay with this, but his eyes told a different story. He clearly hurt, just reliving it. 'In the end, I gave up making plans with my mum. It was easier that way. And I think she was relieved, to be honest. It's not easy to start a new life with a kid hanging round.'

He paused and sighed. 'I always felt like the spare part at her house, like I didn't fit in and that the new guy only tolerated me being there for five minutes then got irritated with me. I'd hate that to happen to Mason.'

So many parallels with his own life. 'I don't know. There are plenty of women happy to have a relationship with a single dad.'

'It's okay. You don't have to be kind.' He laughed. 'I'm not looking for anything. I don't want to get involved in a relationship and have that kind of thing happen again. I'd always be waiting for the ball to drop, right? I'm here to settle my boy and give him a good life. Anything else would be a distraction.'

'But in time?' Why she was asking this and holding her breath waiting for his answer, she didn't know. It wasn't as if she would even be here.

'I haven't really thought about it. But she'd have to be someone very special and someone who was committed to sticking around. The last thing he needs is another person flitting in and out of his life.'

'Of course.' It was suddenly chilly, but strangely there was no breeze. She shivered and stood up. 'It's getting dark. I should go.'

'Okay.' He stood. 'I'll walk you to your truck.'

'You don't have to. I'm perfectly capable of walking a few metres.'

'I know. You're capable of so many things. You're a very impressive woman. But I want to.'

And she wanted him to. Despite everything he was saying about no distractions and not wanting to get involved, and despite her own plans and dreams to leave the island, she didn't want to leave this fireside with the fresh night air, the smoke, the stars and this wonderful, caring man who listened and didn't judge. Whose touch set her alight.

But it was what she had to do, for all their sakes. She pulled herself upright and dug her keys from her shorts pocket. 'Right.'

He walked with her in silence to the truck. Only the sound of their footsteps on gravel and the wekas' night calls rent the air. And yet there was a feeling, a stirring anticipation that seemed to shiver in the atmosphere and shimmer deep inside her, that this wasn't the end, but a beginning. Of a friendship? Yes. She wanted that.

More…? Impossible. He'd just said anything else would be a distraction. And yet…

She pressed the key fob and the truck's lights flashed. She pulled the door open but jumped at the feel of his palm on her hand.

'Carly.'

She turned to face him, her belly dancing with lightness. 'Yes?'

'Thanks again.' He leaned in and pressed a friendly kiss to her cheek.

She closed her eyes as the touch of his skin sent thrills of desire rippling through her. She pulled back, looked at him and caught the heat in his gaze, the need.

She should have turned then and climbed into her truck. She should have driven away into the darkness. But she was transfixed by the way he was looking at her, as if she was…everything.

His previous words about not being distracted seemed to melt from her brain and all she could focus on was his face, his heated eyes, his delicious mouth. So tantalisingly close.

Later, when she thought back to this moment—and she thought back to this moment *a lot*—she wasn't sure how it had happened. One minute they were looking at each other, the next moment they were kissing. Hot, hard and greedy. Desperate. Frantic. Out of control.

The heat of his mouth made her moan and stoked the burning in her belly. She spiked her fingers into his hair and pressed her lips against his, her body hard against his. The outline of his muscled chest pressed against her and, lower, she could feel just how much he was enjoying this. How much he wanted her.

'God, Carly…' His hands cupped her face and held her in place as he captured her bottom lip in his teeth, then took her mouth fully again and kissed her, kissed her and kissed her.

He tasted of hot chocolate and a warm, delicious spice that she couldn't get enough of. He smelt of the smoky fire. He tasted of coming home and of somewhere new, exotic and enticing. Exciting.

It was too much and not enough all at the same time. She didn't want it to end, this night, this kiss lasting for...

Someone committed to staying around.

His words came back to her in a hard jolt of reality. She had an interested buyer visiting tomorrow. A plan to be gone as soon as feasibly possible. So kissing Owen was an impossible and ridiculous idea and a sure-fire way of ruining the fledgling friendship they'd grown.

What on earth was she doing?

'Sorry. I've got to...' She took two shaky steps away from him, jumped into her car and got the hell away.

CHAPTER SIX

'WHO THINKS THIS would be a good spot for a shelter? Let's have a look. There's a good amount of shade from the sun, but also lots of light filtering through the trees, and the ground is nice and flat to lie on. But, before we start to build anything, we have to check to make sure the area is safe. That means looking on the ground and clearing away any wet or rotting debris for a nice, dry sleeping area.'

Carly looked at each of the six Year Eight students in turn, making sure they were listening and engaged. Two of the boys were already on their knees clearing away soggy leaf matter. Two girls were gathering sticks. The other two were staring at her, nodding intently, just as she liked it.

What she didn't like was that her thoughts kept winging back to the other night, to Owen and the kiss. And, even though it had been wonderful, sensual and delicious, she needed to keep her distance from him and rebuild her defences.

'Miss?' One of the boys was staring at her and

she realised she'd lost her train of thought. Or, rather, had found a more pressing one instead of teaching…as she was being paid to do.

'Oh, yes. Right. Keep hold of any long sticks and branches we can use to build the shelter walls. And check overhead to make sure nothing can fall on us in the night.' Six heads turned to look skywards. 'Excellent. Then we have to find a long log we can use as the main shelter strut. Bonus points for finding one with a V-shaped notch in it where we can rest branches and sticks to create a perfect angle for an A-frame shelter.'

A crack of dry wood had her turning to see Wayne, one of the more experienced teachers, running down the hill towards her. His face was pale and he looked shocked. 'Carly, come quickly.'

'What's happened?' She kept her voice and manner calm so the children wouldn't detect any panic. Not that she was panicking. She'd learnt long ago to expect anything and everything by way of incidents on this island. 'What's the matter?'

'There's been an accident.' Wayne's eyebrows rose and his eyes narrowed in a gesture she took to mean *hurry!*

'You can't bring them to me here?' In an emergency situation, she preferred to be closer to the camp if possible, which meant walking wounded should be brought down. That way she could coordinate everything, keep an eye on the camp and be on hand for anything else.

'Yes, she's okay to hobble down here. But, no.'

Which sounded like a lot of confusion to Carly. 'Okay. Kids, I need you to go back to the lecture room and wait for me there. There's a folder with photos of the kind of shelters we're going to build. I'd like you to have a look at them and plan your design for when I get back.' Grabbing the first aid bag she carried with her everywhere, Carly turned to the teacher. 'Okay. Tell me as we walk.'

She followed him at a trot through the bush and up the steep hill behind the bunk rooms, listening to the man's words. 'Tegan and her friends were exploring up by the old mines and she fell onto an old, rusted metal spike. She's got a big gash in her shin that looks quite deep. She's very upset and wouldn't move because she was freaked out by the blood.'

'Right.' Carly stole herself for what she was going to have to deal with. 'There's a lot of it?'

'Not enough to make her weak or need a transfusion, but enough to freak a thirteen-year-old out.'

'Okay. Noted. Don't freak out at the blood.' They turned off the main track and walked towards the Keep Out sign. She pushed the wire fencing down for him to clamber over. 'But why were they here? This place is strictly out of bounds.'

The teacher turned and held the wire for her. 'They were doing the orienteering challenge and got distracted by an adventure.'

She held back her irritation, keeping the lesson about following signs until later, once she'd assessed the patient's mental state.

Which proved to be a good idea, as it turned out, because Tegan was sobbing as they approached. She was propped up against the base of a huge kauri tree trunk, her left leg extended out in front of her, covered in a waterproof jacket. 'I'm… I'm sorry…miss.'

Carly's heart squeezed at the girl's distress. She knelt down to get a good look at the leg injury. 'Hey. Right now, I'm more concerned about your leg than where you are. We'll talk about that later. Can I have a look at the damage?'

The girl's face crumpled again as she sobbed. 'It's nasty. And it hurts.'

'I know, honey. Look away.' Carly glanced up at one of Carly's friends and beckoned her over. 'Pop your arm round Tegan and give her a hug while I have a look.' She peeled back the coat and, sure enough, the wound was wide and deep, and far beyond her skill set. It was still oozing blood, which had also carpeted the ground. 'It looks like you need stitches, and we need to find out if your tetanus injection is up to date. I can manage small wounds, but this is a bit too tricky for me to deal with.'

'Do I have to go...?' There came a stuttering inhaled sob. 'To...hospital?'

'I'm going to let the doctor decide. We'll have to take you over to the island medical centre, unless I can get him to come here. I'll radio in and see if he's free.'

Wayne stepped forward. 'That's a big call. We can take her over there.'

'He has clinic in the morning and then does visits in the afternoons. He could be anywhere on the island right now. But he only lives in the next cove over so he might be closer than we think. I just need to find his whereabouts.'

If I can get over my embarrassment about the kiss. Her cheeks heated as she pulled out the satellite phone and called him.

'Hey, Carly.' His voice was thick with warmth and her body reacted to it with a full-on blush. And heat. So much heat and need. It didn't seem to matter that her head had decided the kiss had been a bad idea, her body wanted more.

It was the first time she'd spoken to him since she'd dashed away on Saturday night. Since the kiss that had been ever-present in her head. She relived his taste, the exquisite press of him in her arms. The way he'd made her feel. All giddy and turned on and discombobulated and yet safe at the same time.

Had made her feel like that. But giving in to their desires had been stupid. She cleared her throat and imbued her tone with as much professionalism and urgency as she could muster. 'Owen, I'm up at the old copper mine site with a young woman. She's got a nasty shin wound from a rusting metal spike and it'll need stitches.'

'Right.' The honey seeped away and his tone relayed a sharp alertness. 'I can be there in twenty. Tetanus status known?'

'No. Can you check, please?' Carly relayed the girl's personal information for him to check on the national vaccination system.

'Okay.' He came back to her. 'I'll have a look. See you *very* soon.'

The way he emphasised 'very' made her heart trip with excitement. 'Sure. We'll get her down to base before you arrive. See you there. Over and out.'

They had to convince Tegan to walk first. And somehow between now and then Carly needed to get her body into line with her head.

After taping some gauze and wadding as a rudimentary compression dressing over the gash, she explained, 'Tegan, I know it's going to be hard for you, and that your leg hurts, but we do need to get you down to the camp.'

'I...don't want...'

'I know. But the sooner we get you there, the sooner we can give you the right pain killers and get you comfortable. Plus, I'll make you some hot chocolate. That makes everything better.' Hot chocolate was always the answer to every woe, as far as Carly was concerned.

The girl gave a sniff, a sob and then a shaky, 'Okay.'

Between them they managed to help Tegan down to the little medical room and wait for Owen's arrival. Carly tried not to watch out for him, instead busying herself with instructions to the little group she'd had to leave earlier, and then double-checking on Tegan and making her a jug of hot chocolate for when Owen had assessed the wound.

And then there he was, striding across the jetty with his medical bag slung over his shoulder. Her heart jolted and jigged and she told herself to stop being silly. They were both professionals. They could deal with an emergency without letting the kiss get in the way.

Couldn't they?

But she wasn't sure how to act around him now. Before...before the kiss...she'd been able to put him into a 'friend' box and a 'colleague' box, but now the edges had all been mussed up and she didn't know how to feel or how to be.

Which explained her shaky hands as she pulled back the temporary dressing to reveal the nasty gash on Tegan's leg.

To his credit, Owen showed little emotional reaction to the wound or the blood as he examined Tegan. 'I'm going to have to do some fancy needlework to get this sorted. But don't worry, I'll try to make it look as good as new.'

'Needlework?' The girl stared up at him.

'Stitches. I'll give you some pain relief first, then I can clean it all up without causing you too much pain.' He drew up some anaesthetic into a syringe and said in a soothing voice, 'Tegan, this is a local anaesthetic. I'm sorry to say it might sting a bit, but then when it starts to work you won't feel a thing.'

He injected the tissue around the wound, explaining everything he did.

'Ow!' Tegan's eyes snapped closed and her face crumpled.

'I know. I'm sorry. You're doing so well, Tegan. This anaesthetic is like magic. Just wait and see.' He waited for her to open her eyes, then held the girl's gaze and smiled, which made her smile back, and made Carly smile too. He was so good with Tegan. He'd been so good with Wiremu and Simon. He was a world-class good guy. And he was still chatting brightly.

He washed his hands and opened a sterile suture pack. Then he slid on some gloves and got Carly to pour saline into a pot before he syringed it over the wound, giving it a thorough clean.

Carly assisted, trying not to catch his eye and willing her trembling hands to settle. Since when had she had shaking hands in response to a man?

Since the man in question was so close, smelt so good and kissed like a god. Too bad the minutes she'd spent trying to align her head and body had come to nothing.

As Owen expertly sewed up the wound, he distracted Tegan with conversation. 'You're going to have an interesting story to tell everyone back home. Talking of... I'll need to have a chat with your parents in a minute. Just to let them know that you've had a little fall and that I'm sorting you out.'

Tegan grimaced. 'My mum will go mad. They'll want to come over and take me home.'

Carly stroked the girl's hand. 'Do you want to go home?'

'No. I want to stay here with my friends.'

Owen's eyebrows rose. 'Are you sure? You won't be able to swim for a few days because of the stitches, and I'm going to have to give you an injection, because your tetanus wasn't up to date. And some antibiotics, in case there were any nasty bugs up there. It's not going to be so fun

just sitting around. Won't home be more comfortable?'

'I don't want to miss out. Can I just sit and watch the others?'

'FOMO. I totally get it,' Carly chipped in. 'But I've got some books you can read if you get bored.'

'I brought some with me. I'm reading the *CHERUB* books again.'

'Brilliant.' Owen grinned and he looked so boyishly handsome and delighted that Carly's heart did a little flip. 'There's nothing like spy stories to take your mind off your leg. So, it's decided then. If your parents are okay with it, I'll check the dressing every day until you go home with the rest of your group.'

'Thank you.' The girl beamed up at him.

'No problem. Just don't go off-piste next time. Stick to the path.' His tone became just a tad more assertive. 'Stick to the rules.'

'I'm sorry.' Tegan looked at Owen and then at Carly. 'I'm so sorry, Carly.'

'I know you are.' Carly didn't feel much like telling the girl off now, especially given that Owen had handled it so well. 'Off-piste' was the perfect way to describe the side trip to the mine. 'Here's your hot chocolate. Sit here for a while and drink it. Dr Cooper will chat to your parents.'

Carly took the opportunity to leave them to the

call. It had been an easier interaction with Owen than she'd expected but she definitely needed to get away from him.

She was just finishing up outside the lecture room with the shelter group when she saw him striding across the grass towards her. Her heart hammered against her ribcage. What was he going to say? How did he feel about the kiss? What did he want from her?

What did she want from him?

The answer to every question was simple and difficult at the same time. She just didn't know. Apart from the jittery heart and excitement rolling in her tummy, of course…she knew about that. And the desire to kiss him again. And the many, many reasons why she shouldn't.

She clapped her hands to get her students' attention. 'Okay, everyone. We're finished here. Well done for some great ideas. Go wash up for lunch.'

'Carly.' Owen's tone was friendly, but his manner was…she couldn't describe it…apprehensive?

'Hey. Thanks for coming over so quickly.' Her mouth suddenly felt dry. Everything felt stuttered and difficult compared to the other night, with marshmallows, hot chocolate, the glowing fire and the magic of his mouth. 'Apparently Tegan was upset by all the blood but you put her at ease. You've got a friend for life there, Dr Cooper.'

'I'll make sure to come and check her dressings tomorrow.' He frowned. 'How come there's bits of rusting metal around the island?'

Oh...that was what he wanted to talk about. She almost sagged in relief. She knew they had to address the kiss, but she wasn't sure she was brave enough to do it right now. 'It's from old mining machinery and it's impossible to move, I'm afraid. A lot of it has been absorbed into the landscape. Nature has almost subsumed it and few people even know it's there. But I'll make sure I put up a bigger sign and more barbed-wire fencing. There's always something.'

'Good.' There was a pause. He shoved his hand deep into his pocket then looked right at her. 'Look, Carly, I think we need to have a quick chat.'

And she knew exactly what it would be about. But he was right; they needed to sort out their boundaries whether she was brave enough or not. 'Okay. You'd better come over to the house.'

He hadn't even known he was going to say those words until they'd tumbled from his mouth. It had been easy to talk to her with the buffer of an emergency between them, and he could have just waved goodbye and got back into his boat, but that would have been the coward's way out. They'd stepped over a line and they needed to deal with it. Even if he felt tongue-tied and off-balance.

He was not sure about going over to her house, being surrounded by her things and her scent, being alone with Carly. Every minute spent away from her was a torture of needing to see her again, railing against his decision not to. Every second spent with her made that decision fade into nothing.

Truth was, he was smitten, and he didn't know how to cope with that. His relationship with Miranda must have started with a little smitten-ness, but he couldn't remember it. 'Don't you need to get back to your students?'

'No. It's fine. I'm finished for the day now. Like you, I tend to have structured stuff in the mornings then wing the afternoons.' A little frown hovered over her eyes as they strolled to her house, and he wondered what she was really thinking behind all this small talk. 'This afternoon the teachers and kids are going for a hike over to the Mansion House for a history lesson, so I'm going to do paperwork.'

'I've never managed to get to the Mansion House.'

'Oh, you should.' The frown lines smoothed out a little. 'It's a beautiful old colonial building and used regularly as a wedding venue. There are

lots of photos of the island over the years chart-
ing its history.'

'I should take Mason.'

'He'd love it. You can either walk over the hill
or take the boat round—there's plenty of moor-
ing, and a little cafe with home baking and the
best ice-cream on the island. And a lovely beach
to cool off with a swim, if it's a hot day. All quite
safe.'

Safe. That was what this conversation was. Polite, well-mannered and avoiding the very thing
they should be talking about.

The inside of her cottage was cosy and homely,
with well-worn furniture and what looked like
hand-made knitted throws in rich blues and subtle
reds. It was a home, unlike the place he was living
in. Mason needed a home. Owen made a mental
note to add soft furnishings to his next online
shopping list. Not something he'd ever thought
he'd give a damn about, but he could see how they
added softness and comfort. Mason needed that.

Carly led him into the kitchen and put the kettle
on. He watched as she gracefully moved around
her space. She was dressed in the short shorts
for teaching, hiking and water sports, which he
now knew to be her work outfit, along with a blue
T-shirt with the bright yellow Camp Rāwhiti logo
above her heart. The sunlight streaming through
the big bay window caught the red in her hair,

making him transfixed. She turned and gave him a hesitant smile as she dropped tea bags into two cups.

His gaze landed on her lips and, even though he knew their conversation had to be about not kissing, it was the only thing he wanted to do right now. So, he avoided the subject altogether. 'How did it go with the buyer?'

Her smile wavered and she shrugged. 'I don't think she was interested. She certainly hasn't put an offer in or anything.'

'Is that good or bad?'

'It's frustrating, to be honest. I feel like I'm in limbo.'

So did he—caught somewhere between his warring heart and head. If he'd been free and not a father, he might have gone with his heart and suggested a fling before she left. But he wasn't free, he had a child to think about. The spectre of the kiss hung over them and if he didn't say anything it'd always be there.

He took a deep breath and exhaled slowly. 'Look, Carly. I'm so sorry, after what I said about not wanting a distraction. I shouldn't have kissed you.'

Her cheeks pinked and she gave him a hurried nod. 'No. Well, yes. I mean, I kissed you first, I think. And I'm sorry too. I was out of order.'

'I think we both got carried away with the

lovely night sky and the marshmallows and the fire.'

'Yes.' She poured hot water into the mugs and didn't give him any more eye contact, but she said, 'It's something, isn't it? This thing we've got going.'

'This thing we're not going to act on.'

'Yes. That thing.' She finally lifted her head and looked at him, and he could see the same struggle he was experiencing mirrored in her eyes. He could see lightness and some darkness, need and affection, confusion, hope and regret... But nothing had really happened between them apart from the kiss. And yet, it felt as if something was happening.

Her eyebrows rose. 'It's weird. I haven't wanted to kiss another man since Raff died, and yet here I am, wanting to do it again, even though I'm leaving and I won't be back for a long time. If ever. Well, I will come back, obviously, because Mia and Harper are here, but you know what I mean... I'm going. You're staying. You've got Mason. I've got plans.'

Wow. He hadn't expected all that. It was a revelation and a responsibility. A revelation, because he hadn't expected her to say something so honest. And a responsibility, because the first kiss after something so traumatic as losing your husband had to be perfect. Symbolic or something, he imagined. Was that why she'd run off—because it hadn't been perfect? Because he wasn't Raff? Because it was too soon, too much?

He wasn't sure how to react, because she'd just admitted she wanted to do it again and they really shouldn't. 'It's just a physical thing, I think. Two people on their own and all that. I know I sometimes feel kind of lonely.' Now he just sounded like a loser. 'Well, not lonely. Alone. You know how it is.'

But she smiled again. 'Yes. *Alone*. That's exactly right. Which is fine, until it isn't. Some days you don't even notice the silence, and some days it's deafening and you just want someone to talk to, right? Like this.'

'Like this.' Except, he was probably making a mess of it all. 'Okay. So we're both agreed—it can't happen again.'

'Agreed. Let's drink to it. No kissing.' She handed him a mug of steaming tea and they clinked cups together. 'You have my permission to stop me if I make a move.'

He laughed, grateful they could both see the funny side of this—even though it did nothing to erase the torment and deep ache to spend more time with her. He was relieved, too, that it was a mutual thing and he wasn't dreaming it. 'Back at you, Carly. I mean, I can control myself. It's just hard around you.'

'I'm not sure we should even say things like that.' She pressed her lips together, but the smile spread across her face. Heat and need hit her eyes. 'But I'm glad you did. And I'm glad I'm not the only one feeling it.'

'We'll just have to stick to a hands-off, mutual appreciation society.'

'A mutual appreciation society.' She giggled. 'Yes. That's what it is. At least we can laugh about it. In another life, we might have made something of it, right?'

He ached to make something of it right now. To touch her again, to kiss her. To make love to her right here in this kitchen. The only thing he could do was keep his distance until she left. 'I'd say so. Yes.'

'Bad timing, then.' She shrugged, looking up at him through impossibly long eyelashes. 'You're a good guy, Owen Cooper.'

'Which goes to show how little you know me.' He took a sip of tea to stop himself from saying any more, or something he might regret.

Because in another life, where Carly was concerned, he'd have preferred to be very bad indeed.

CHAPTER SEVEN

'Mia! Yoo-hoo!' Without knocking, as always, Carly rushed into her sister-in-law's house and found her in the kitchen, sudsy hands in the deep, battered sink, baby Harper in her high chair, her cherub face smudged with something that looked like yoghurt. Carly slicked a kiss on her niece's head and then caught Mia's gaze. 'We need to talk.'

'And good morning to you too.' Mia wiped her hands on a tea towel. 'Sure. What about?'

About the camp. About my crazy, mixed-up feelings for your boss. About a mind-warping kiss...

'The estate agent just called me. The woman that viewed last weekend has more questions. I think...' Carly's tummy fluttered with nerves, excitement and a smattering of anxiety. 'I think she's going to put an offer in.'

'Wow.' Mia's eyes grew large and sparkly. 'I thought she wasn't interested.'

'Me too. When she was here, she played disinterested, but she's keen. Apparently, she was asking about resource consent for multiple dwellings.'

'Multiple?'

'Apartments, probably.' Carly imagined towering blocks and a busy resort-style feel to the haven she'd come to love. Her heart contracted.

Mia frowned. 'Oh. I see. Well, we can't do much about that. But I guess it's good news if she's asking questions like that.'

'Is it good news, though?' They'd come to the truth of the matter now. 'Apartments. Holiday lets. I imagine there'll be a swimming pool and a bar. It's not exactly the legacy your parents wanted.'

'We can't dictate how someone's going to use the land once we've sold it.'

'I know. I wish we could. At least some of it is covenanted, so a decent acreage will remain bush.'

'Oh, honey.' Mia wrapped her arms round Carly's shoulder and gave her a tight hug. 'Do not beat yourself up about this. Things move on. Change is the only constant. I grew up at the camp, and I don't feel bad about selling it, so you shouldn't.'

'Are you sure?' Because, even though Mia was saying the words, there was something in her eyes that gave Carly pause. She just hoped her friend wasn't saying all the right things just to make her feel better about leaving. 'It's your family home.'

Mia shrugged. 'I know and, to be honest, it does feel strange to know it's not going to be there any more. But I'm a single mum, and on a nurse's salary I don't get to save much. I need to be able to set Harper up with a college fund and selling the camp will do that.'

'College? She's not even two years old. If she's got any sense she'll be a builder...there's so much development going on here, she'll have a job for life.' Carly jokily pumped her pecs but then saw the anxiety in Mia's expression. Then she glanced round the kitchen, noticing that the unit doors were cracked and the walls needed a coat of paint...in fact, the cute cottage needed an overhaul, something that would cost time and money Mia didn't have. She needed this sale to go through. 'But I totally understand. It must be hard being Mum and Dad and the only breadwinner.'

Carly had grown up used to being on her own, but losing her whole family in one accident must have changed Mia's outlook for ever. Change might be the only constant, but it was clear the woman needed to feel secure and to provide enough for her daughter, just in case anything should happen.

And now Carly felt torn apart. Should she stay here for Mia and Harper—be their constant?

But Mia squeezed her tightly again before letting her go and focusing back on the sudsy water. 'I may be a child of the camp, but I'm also a parent, and I would never, ever expect Harper to do anything just because I wanted her to do it, or because of my legacy—whatever that means. Please don't spend your life doing things just because they'd make my parents happy.'

'And Raff.' Carly's chest hurt at the thought of her late husband. She wanted always to make him proud.

'Of course. Yes. And Raff.' Mia smiled sadly. 'My brother would want, more than anything, for you to be happy. To have a future and a family. And to travel, just like you both planned to do. He wouldn't want you to be sad for ever.'

'I'm not.' Carly dug deep for a smile and thought about the last few days of confusion, attraction and excitement. 'At least, not all the time.'

'Particularly not when you're with the good doctor?' Mia's eyes twinkled and she pretended to swoon.

'Who? Owen?' Just thinking about him brought heat to Carly's cheeks, and other places that had no business getting heated. 'There's nothing happening there.'

'Hmm.' Mia's gaze focused on Carly's face. 'I mean, what's not to like? The man's a great doctor. And very resourceful. He's not complained once about having no receptionist while Anahera's away, and he's dealt with all the messages coming through to the surgery every day, even the mundane stuff. And I saw him doing DIY the other day when I went to drop Mason off at home. That man looks good in a sweat.' She wafted her hand in front of her face, as if suddenly hot.

Carly wished she'd seen him in a sweat, but wasn't going to admit that to her sister-in-law. 'Still nothing happening. If he's that perfect, why don't you make a play for him?' Then she winced, wishing she hadn't said that. She didn't like the idea of Owen being with another woman.

But Mia shook her head. 'Not my type.'

'Oh?' Good. And also interesting... Mia had never spoken about the kind of guy she might be attracted to. 'Which is?'

'I don't have one. And this isn't about me.' Mia eyed Carly with suspicion. 'Do you know what parents are really, really good at?'

'What?'

'Knowing when someone is lying to them. There's something with the doctor...right?' She pierced Carly with a steely stare that almost had her spitting out the truth.

We kissed. It was good. I want more kisses... maybe more other things. But everything's confusing. 'He's a nice guy.'

'He is. So, tell me, is the wobble about the sale only because of my parents' legacy or is there more to it? Because you don't have to sell. You don't have to go travelling. You could stay a while, see how things develop.'

'I really, really do need to go. I need to get my head straightened out, and I can't do it with the memories of the camp and now Owen blurring everything. I have to have some space.'

'So he's in the picture?' Mia looked hopeful.

'No. But he's stopping me looking at things with a clear head.'

'Okay. I get that. Men, huh?'

'And what do you know about that? You haven't dated for years.' It was gentle ribbing, although Carly thought it was high time Mia started to date again. Did she feel alone sometimes too?

'Because of men. Huh?' Mia laughed and rolled her eyes. 'Seriously, though, talk to me any time. I'm here for you.' She grabbed a wash-cloth, ran it under the sink, squeezed it out and then handed it to Carly. 'Now, would you please wipe Harper's face while I finish the washing up? I'm taking Harper and Mason to the beach for a play date and I'm late already. There's some apple and feijoa pie in the fridge, if you're hungry. You're getting too thin. Eat, woman.'

'Sounds lovely, but I'm fine. Thanks.'

She wasn't, though. She wasn't fine at all. She

was all muddled up and desperately wanted someone to talk things through with all over again.

It was no use. Keeping his distance from Carly
was impossible on this small island when their
lives and those of the people around them were
so intertwined. He saw her when she called in
to see Mia at the medical centre, while lunching
at the yacht club and bumped into her in the tiny
supermarket. They waved as their boats zipped
past each other across the glittering bay. Everywhere he turned, she was there. And alongside
that came the crushing craving to get to know her
better, despite everything they'd said.

It had been almost a week since their 'mutual
appreciation society' agreement and the ache
hadn't dimmed. In fact, if anything, it had grown
stronger.

But right now the only thing he needed to
do was put her out of his head and write up his
notes from this morning's surgery. Then review
the messages on the answer-machine, chase up
blood results and go on his afternoon visits…
Who had said coming to a tiny island would be
easier doctoring? Not to mention fixing up the
cottage, which he tried to do in the little spare
time he had when not looking after Mason.

But he couldn't concentrate today. His last conversation with Carly kept coming back to him, resonating deep inside.

Alone.

He hadn't realised he felt like that.

When Miranda had left, he'd felt lost and totally out of his depth, but in some ways it had been a relief to end the struggle between them and accept things weren't working. He'd been thrown into sole care of their son, and he'd floundered, asking for advice from anyone and everyone about how to deal with a devastated child. His focus had been only on Mason.

Sure, he'd chatted about the failure of his marriage to his friends, but he hadn't looked for anyone else to fill the gap Miranda had left. Certainly, he hadn't had the headspace for someone else in his life. But, now things were settling, he noticed the space more.

It would be even larger when Carly left.

The door to his consultation room flew open and a woman's voice made him jump. 'Doc? Are you in here? Ah, yes. *Kia Ora*, Owen.'

'Anahera? You're back?' He jumped up and gave her a quick hug. 'Am I pleased to see you.'

'I'm pleased to be here.' She grinned. 'But I've heard you've been coping just fine without me.'

'Barely.' He pointed to the piles of paperwork he'd been wading through and the filing he'd put off because he didn't know the system well enough yet. 'I'm drowning under bits of paper. How's Wiremu?'

She shrugged but smiled. 'He's okay. A bit wobbly, but getting there. Try telling that man to slow down. He doesn't know the meaning of the word.'

The ringing of the reception phone interrupted her and her eyebrows rose. 'Not even in the office for five minutes and it starts.'

Owen laughed. 'The island gossip machine knows you're here already.'

'Honey, I *am* the island gossip machine!' she bellowed as she disappeared down the corridor.

Laughing and relieved that he now had an extra pair of hands to run the surgery, he went back to reviewing his notes. But the door swung open again. Anahera. 'We've got a boat versus jet-ski accident in the harbour. There's a head injury and some minor scrapes, by all accounts.'

'Just as I thought things would start to quieten down. There's no rest for the wicked.' He just wished he'd a chance to be wicked…with Carly. He slid his chair back and grabbed his bag. 'Tell them I'm on my way.'

She nodded. 'I'll try to find Carly and get her to join you at the harbour.'

'Great. Thanks.' *I think.* But working with her would be no different from passing her in the street, with a quick nod of the head and focus elsewhere, right?

Wrong.

The head injury victim was lying prone on the harbour causeway, apparently having collapsed after jumping off his boat. He had a nasty cut on his forehead and a lumpy bruise blooming around his eye socket. The jet-ski rider was nursing what looked like a dislocated shoulder and a grudge against the boat owner, given the stream of curse words coming out of his mouth, but Owen had assessed priority and was attending to the semi-conscious head injury patient first. If jet-ski man was shouting and cursing, he was at least conscious.

He was stabilising the collapsed man's neck and head when Carly came bounding along the jetty. The moment she swung into view, his heart stumbled over itself. He tried to convince himself that he was just relieved to have someone else's help to deal with the incident, but he knew it was more than that. 'Hey, Carly.'

'Hey. What have we got here?' She knelt next to their injured man, across from Owen, and her scent swirled around him, sending his memory spiralling to their kiss. The fire. The moment of true connection.

It was good she was leaving. It was. Then he'd be able to focus wholly on the things he needed to focus on. Like on the job in hand, and not on how great she smelt. 'Head injury. He's slipping in and out of consciousness. Glasgow coma score of twelve but fluctuating.'

'Okay.' She pulled out her satellite phone from her backpack. 'Have you radioed in for an evacuation?'

'Not yet. I've only just got here.'

'What about the other guy?' She crooked her neck towards the jet-ski rider who was propped up against the wooden fencing that edged the top of the causeway. He'd stopped cursing and now looked shocked and hunched in pain as he held his left arm tight against his side.

'Could you assess him? Looks like a dislocated shoulder. If it is, he'll need a sling to immobilise it. If he's in too much pain for you to touch it, we can swap jobs and I'll give him some inhaled anaesthetic while you keep this neck stable.'

'Sure thing. I'll just radio for an evac. One or two passengers?' She frowned and he saw then that her eyes were puffy and her cheeks blotchy, as if she'd been crying.

He glanced over to the jet-ski rider then back to Carly. 'Two. Are you okay?'

Her reddened eyes widened in surprise. 'Sure. Why?'

'You look upset.'

She blinked and shook her head quickly, as if

to tell him, *not here*. 'I'm radioing in. Then I can stabilise this man's neck if you want to administer pain relief to the other guy.'

'Later, then.'

She looked as if she was going to say no, but her shoulders sagged and she nodded. 'Actually, I could do with a chat.'

It gave him a sharp punch of pride to his chest that she trusted him enough not to pretend she was okay and considered him someone she could talk to. He had to be that person—her person. The friend she needed.

He nodded and caught her gaze—and there it was again…the invisible but tangible connection that seemed to pull them closer and closer. For the tiniest moment, she smiled.

He smiled back.

Then he focused on their patients.

The next hour was a blur of activity, stabilising the injuries, handing over to the paramedics, clearing up the debris from the flurry of open sterile packs and oxygen tubing. Then a quick debrief in the yacht club that he'd tried to turn down but had been unable to, because Wiremu's son, Nikau, had come out and wrapped them both in a bear hug, thanking them for saving his father's life and insisting on buying them a drink.

And now it was just the two of them, standing outside the yacht club on the deck overlooking the moorings, finally alone, the chaos subsiding… apart from the chaos in his chest whenever he was close to Carly. 'So, how are you doing now?'

She turned to look at him, clearly understanding what he was alluding to. 'Okay, thanks. I was just having a wobble.'

'About?'

'Life in general.' She laughed ruefully.

'You want to chat now?'

She looked at a group of locals walking towards them and shook her head. 'Not here. Can we go somewhere else?'

'Absolutely.' He put his hand on her arm then took it away. Where did the boundaries between friends who were attracted to each other, but who'd also sworn off anything physical, start and end? Could he touch her?

He forced himself to shove his hands into his pockets and looked up the road to the start of a trail that disappeared into the bush. 'I haven't explored that track. You want to go for a walk?'

She looked towards the trail head and then back to him again. 'Yes. Actually, I do.'

She set off walking hard and fast, as if she was trying to get away from something. He hoped it wasn't him, but she stopped every now and then to make sure he was there. She didn't say anything, and he took her lead. When she was ready, she'd talk.

Whatever was eating her fuelled her pace as they wound deeper and higher through the bush. When he reached the top of the hill, he found her bent double, red-cheeked and breathing raggedly.

'You're hard on yourself. That's one heck of a climb,' he managed as he hauled a lungful of fresh air into his lungs.

'I like the way I feel after… I've got to…the top.' She panted and plopped onto a wooden bench—this one had no engraved plaque on it. 'Not during it.'

'Have you exorcised your demons yet?'

'Is that what it looked like? I was just seeing if you could keep up with me.' She giggled, the bubbly sound a salve to his ears. He hated seeing her anything but happy.

'And clearly I can. Any time.'

'Oh, yeah?' Her eyes sparked. The puffiness was starting to subside but there were traces left. 'You want me to show you how fast I can move through the bush?'

The roots…the branches…he wasn't as familiar as her with this terrain. He was bound to lose. He put his hands up and winced. 'Maybe another time.'

'Coward.'

'Yes.' He grinned and sat next to her, then raised his head and looked through a gap in the huge kauri trees. 'Wow.'

Below them was a beautiful bay of glittering turquoise water and white sand beaches. At one end of the bay was a huge white colonial villa that dominated the promontory. 'The Mansion House?'

'Yes. Isn't it lovely? They don't build houses like that any more.'

'Probably no double glazing. It'd be freezing in the winter.'

'Ah, come on. Where's the romance, Owen? It's beautiful, with its sweeping verandas and all that dainty filigree carving.'

'How is keeping warm unromantic? If it's too cold, you're not going to want to take your clothes off.'

'Oh, trust me. You would with the right person.' She started to laugh, and he was mesmerised by the sound that made his body heat and his chest warm.

He also didn't miss the way she'd looked at him as she'd said those words, as if he just might have been the right person once upon a time, in a different life. It was a joke and a dare and, not for the first time, he wondered how she would look naked. Under him. Straddling him.

A crackle of dry leaves and snapping branches had him on alert and turning his head, although the adrenalin of desire still rippled through him. There, a few feet away from them, was… He blinked. *Really?* 'What the hell is that? A kangaroo? Tell me I'm dreaming, or did we just go through some weird travel portal and end up in Australia?'

She laughed softly and bent towards the animal, her hand outstretched, whispering, 'It's a wallaby. There are a few wild ones in the bush.'

'How come? They're not indigenous to New Zealand.'

They both watched as it hopped away into the dense bushes. 'By all accounts, years ago an old governor general imported all sorts of exotic animals and plants to see which would thrive and what flora and fauna the land would be useful for. Most things didn't survive, but the wallabies thrived. Unfortunately, they destroy the wildlife and vegetation, so we've got trappers to catch them and re-home them in a more suitable environment. But I have to admit, they're cute and add a quirkiness to the place. The kids love them if they get a glimpse. We only have a few left now.'

'Is there anywhere more wonderful than Rāwhiti Island?' As soon as he said it, he wished he could take the words back, because her face had grown sad again.

'I hope there are lots more wonderful places all over the world, and I intend to visit them all.'

'Oh, there are many, Carly, and you'll have an amazing time.' His chest hurt to say this and to be positive about her leaving, but he really hoped she did have the best adventure. 'Someone once gave me a *One Hundred Places to Visit Before You Die* book. I think I've still got it somewhere in one of the boxes that finally arrived last week. You can borrow it, if you like.'

'Are you trying to get rid of me?' Smiling, she raised her knees up, anchoring her feet on the bench and wrapping her arms round her shins.

'Just helping you fulfil your dream. And yet… you don't look too excited about it all.'

'Well, it's rushing at me now.' She inhaled deeply and let out slowly. 'We've had an offer on the camp.'

'Oh?'

'She wants to turn it into apartments. I'm not sure how I feel about it not being a camp any more.' She gave a shrug. 'Mia says I need to get over myself.'

'What will the schools do if they can't come here?'

'We're not unique. There are plenty of camp options across the country for them to choose from.'

'So that's not what's got you rethinking? What aren't you happy about the sale?'

'Well, I am happy, of course. It was the plan. And there again, no. I'm wobbling.' She chuckled but it was tinged with something else. Anxiety? Regret? 'Sorry, I'm not making any sense.'

'Far from it. When Miranda and I split up, I didn't know if it was the right thing for any of us. It was a relief to end the arguing and struggles, but I had no idea how I was going to manage or how Mason would react to his mum leaving. And, when I sold up to come here, I didn't know if it was the most ridiculous idea in the world. Giving up everything for the unknown is not just exciting but unsettling too.'

'I'm so glad you understand. Everyone else is all about the "live your best life while you have the chance" and they don't understand why I'm apprehensive. Of course I'm excited. But the excitement's all tangled up with other emotions too. I'm not sad about leaving, so much as drawing a line under everything. I guess I feel a bit overwhelmed that it's finally happening.'

'You don't have to go anywhere, right? You could stay.' Was that the wrong thing to say?

It was a *selfish* thing to say. Life on the island would be just a little bit less bright without her here, but he couldn't ask her stay for him. What was he even thinking? No one ever stayed around for him.

'Mia said that too. And I know it sounds stupid, and I'm not making any sense, but I feel like I owe it to myself to go.' She jumped up from the bench and waited for him to follow, then they started to wind their way back down the path. 'Plus, Mia won't say anything, but she needs the money. The sale will set her and Harper up for life.'

Owen frowned. 'I didn't know she was in financial trouble.'

'It's not that exactly. She's getting by. But after everything she's been through—losing all her family—she deserves a bit more than just getting by, right?'

'I'll see if I can do more to help her. She's babysitting Mason right now. Maybe I should pay her?'

'God, no. Don't do that.' Carly put her palm up. 'She'd be mortified. She's happy for Harper to have a friend. Just return the favour every now and then and have Harper over to play—give Mia some space to have some me time.'

He wondered what exactly that was, because he hadn't had any for a very long time. 'We've barely had time to breathe since Anahera was called away, but I'll make sure I help her more.'

She slowed and looked up at him, a smile on her lips. 'I knew you would. Look after her for me.'

It sounded so final. 'You haven't gone yet.'

'But soon. Selling the camp is good for her, but that's the end of that part of my life. I keep telling myself that everything that happened to me before Raff was preparing me for his death.'

'Living in foster care must have given you a lot of resilience, but even so, no one should go through what you did, moving from place to place.' And yet here she was, planning to do it again.

Her walking pace picked up. 'I don't know about resilience. Being uplifted time after time hurts. I mean, really hurts. You try to settle in, watch to see how everyone in the family acts, what roles they have…what kind of dynamic is in the house. You mould yourself to fit into it, you take on a role…the clever one, the funny one, the quiet one. Mainly, I was the quiet one, observing, trying not to trip up and do something stupid and be moved on. But I was always moved on eventually, for one reason or another.'

His heart squeezed at the thought of a little Carly, someone Mason's age, trying to fit herself into a new space, then another, then another. 'That must have been so hard for you.'

'You learn to become self-reliant, in the end. To block off the feelings. To not get emotionally involved in case you lose it all again. Because it's exhausting, trying to rebuild and to survive. But then I met Raff and came here and I settled in straight away. There was no role to take, other than to be myself, even though I didn't know who that was. Who that *is*. I belonged here, I was part of something…and I didn't get moved on, but the family did. And I was left all alone again. I mean, sure I have Mia and Harper. But I wake up alone every morning and go to bed alone every night. I make the decisions here. I'm the boss of a place I never asked for, in a job I never applied for. And now… I don't know what I want.'

'You'll work it out.'

'I hope so.' She smiled, raising her eyebrows.

'You're pretty special. You don't need to go anywhere to see that.'

'Thank you. Wow, that's kind.'

He stopped walking and turned to face her. 'It's not kind, Carly. It's honest. You're stunning. Beautiful. Strong.'

'Not strong, just bloody minded. Trust me, it's taken a long time for me to be able to talk about Raff and his parents in the past tense.'

'You must have felt as if your whole world was ripped apart.'

She nodded. 'But I have to move on, and I think that means I have to leave. To be honest, I'm so confused, but I think I can only find out who I am if I'm not here. I'm excited and a bit daunted to find out.'

'I can't wait to see who Carly Edwards is when she comes back, because I'm not sure she can get any better than who she is right now.'

If she came back at all. Which should have been a shrill warning alarm, yet made part of him want to deep-dive into getting to know her while he had the chance.

He took in her bright eyes that always reflected her emotions. She was honest, deep to her core. The beautiful mouth tasted so fine. But it wasn't her physicality that appealed as much as the person she was. Deep-down good. A fighter. Endearing. Funny. Beautiful. And mixed-up, too. And that made her even more perfect. She wasn't trying to be someone else, or to put on a brave face, she was living through uncertainty and admitting she felt lost sometimes.

Didn't everyone? But not everyone was open enough to say it out loud.

Her gaze snagged his and for a few beats they just looked at each other. So much passed between them. Understanding. Compassion. Need. Heat.

He couldn't take his eyes off her. He didn't want her to leave. He wanted to get to know her better. Wanted to make love to her, to share parts of his life with her. Explore something new together.

This was crazy mixed-up. He was crazy mixed-up.

But she still held his gaze.

He took a step closer to her and she closed the

gap, reaching for him and wrapping her arms around his waist, leaning her head against his chest and holding on.

He stroked her hair, closed his eyes and fought every instinct to kiss her. This was what she needed, just the hug, nothing more.

But when she pulled away she was breathing heavily, her eyes misted. He put his palm to her cheek and she curled into his touch.

'Thanks, Owen. You're a good listener. And a fine hugger.'

He dropped his hand from her face, wondering how wise it was to be honest. Probably not wise at all, but he did it anyway. 'I want to kiss you. I want to make you feel better about everything.'

'We can't. It'll make everything too complicated.' She curled her fingers into his. 'But I already feel better. Thank you. Just having someone to listen really helps.'

'Sure. Any time.' He squeezed her hand then let go.

It always seemed to be like this with her—an opening of their hearts, an acceptance of each other's desires and all the reasons not to act on them. It helped that it was so honest and yet it didn't help at all. Because what was the point in telling someone your deepest desires if you couldn't act on them? Might as well keep them locked inside.

And then there was Mason, who was as soft on her as Owen was. Who didn't need any more confusion.

This was crazy. This wasn't about Mason. This was about himself. His concern for Mason getting too close to Carly was a deflection or, indeed, a reflection of getting too close to her himself. He knew all about women leaving; his mother had done it and his wife too.

Carly had good reasons. Hell, they'd all had good reasons to pursue the life they wanted and deserved. He was just tired of being the fall guy. He needed to focus on the kind of life he wanted. Like Carly, he wasn't sure what that was yet, except creating security for Mason.

He quickly stepped back. 'I have to go.'

Carly blinked, shocked. 'Did I say something wrong?'

'No. It's me. I have a habit of wanting things I can't have and all that leads to is a headache and a lot of stress.'

'So you're running away.' She laughed, but it was gentle and sad. The words stung but he couldn't deny the truth.

'Yes. Actually, I am. I'm going to pop by Mia's and pick up my boy, then take him on an adventure, the way we planned when we decided to come here.'

Then he pivoted away from her and started to jog down the hill, in exactly the opposite direction from Carly.

CHAPTER EIGHT

SHE SHOULD HAVE cancelled the kayaking, but then what would that have taught little Mason—that adults made promises and didn't keep them? That wasn't a lesson he needed to learn at four years old.

Hell, she'd had enough life lessons growing up to make her protective of any child, but for some reason her heart had made space for this little boy.

She found a smile for Mason, who was standing in front of her in a cute short wetsuit with a shark on the front, and a huge, excited grin. 'Right then, buddy. First off, we need to lift the kayak down to the water.'

'I'll take one end...you take the other.' Owen stepped in and picked up one end of the bright orange kayak, his manner clipped and assertive.

He'd been right, of course, when he'd said he needed to focus on having a wonderful life filled with adventures with his son, but watching him jog away from her the other day had made her chest contract with hurt and confusion. He hadn't even pretended he was running for any other reason.

I have a habit of wanting things I can't have.

He wanted her, despite everything. And he had been willing to say it. And she wanted him too, which threw everything about her plans into upheaval. Should she stay, just in case something came of this attraction?

No. She couldn't put all her hopes and dreams into this man. She needed to grow and explore the world.

And was it her imagination, or was he being standoffish today? His gaze wasn't quite so intense as usual, his smile not as full.

He was closing himself off.

She couldn't blame him. She was struggling with her emotions too. Spending time with him just made her want more of him…more time, more kisses. She'd do well to take a leaf from his book and keep her distance…as far as she could, when giving them a personal kayak lesson.

'Thanks. Mason, you bring the oars.' She showed him how to carry them, hoping that focusing on the child would keep her from focusing too much on the man.

Of course, it didn't work. Even with them in a separate kayak she was too aware of Owen's strong hands, his powerful stroke, the tightening and relaxing of his muscles. Which were far too prevalent, given that the man was bare-chested save for the life jacket she'd insisted they all wear.

She took them across the bay to explore the mangroves, pointing to the little shoals of jumping fish and the stingrays swimming languidly in the shallows.

Mason's face broke into a huge smile as he watched the large flat shapes moving beneath the water. 'What are they doing?'

'They're feeding on the little sea worms, insects and shrimps.'

'They eat insects?' His eyes widened.

'Sea insects, yes.'

Mason pulled a face. 'Yukky!'

'You don't want to eat insects?'

'No way. I like ice-cream and marshmallows.'

'Good choice.' As she watched the little boy's amusement grow as large as his eyes, she realised she was falling for him too.

What on earth was she doing, spending more time with them? It was like an addiction. Instead of putting distance between herself and this little family, she gave herself excuses and reasons to see them. She just craved more and more.

She smiled over at them both and realised Mason was starting to shiver. 'Right, we should probably get back. The wind's picking up and it's getting cold. Last one back to camp makes the hot chocolate.'

'Hey, not fair, you're a fantastic kayaker.' Owen put his oar in and splashed cold water over her. It was the first time today that his face had broken a smile.

'Hey!' She splashed back. 'There's two of you against one of me. That's an unfair advantage right there.' Not just for kayaking but for an arrow of longing straight to her chest.

'It helps if the two of us both row at the same time and in the same direction,' Owen yelled and then started some seriously frenzied rowing.

By the time she reached the shore, men and boat were back up in the boathouse. Owen sauntered back and took the end of her kayak to carry it up. 'Mason's hooked. It looks like I'm going to have to add a kayak to my list of things to buy.'

'Look no further. We have to sell off everything here.'

'Good call. I expect mates' rates.' He turned to look at her and she couldn't read his expression.

But she felt a tight twist in her gut. It was like being on a roller coaster…fun, laughter and the looming end. The push and pull of attraction and the struggle. And the excitement. Oh, the excitement of it all. 'I'll talk to Mia and see if we can come to a deal.'

Mason was still shivering as he helped them stack the kayaks and hose them down. She stroked his head. 'Hey, buddy. You look cold. Go up to the house and have a nice warm shower.'

But Owen frowned, back to standoffishness after that glimpse of warmth. 'We can just use the one in the bunk house.'

'Ah, I'd prefer it if you didn't. I've just cleaned it in preparation for the next group.'

'We'll just have one at home.'

Why was he stalling about going into her house? 'The boy's cold, Owen. Use mine.'

He caught her gaze, his eyes boring into her soul. 'Okay. And then we'll be on our way.'

Owen hoisted Mason into his arms and sped through the house, trying not to linger. It felt intensely personal here, surrounded by Carly's things. There was no evidence of any other person, apart from the photo of her wedding day in the hallway. She looked so happy, a certain sort of sparkle in eyes he'd yet to see—true joy.

God, he wished that for her more than anything. But not at the cost of losing his heart. Again. Hadn't he already learnt that, when it came to women, he had absolutely no clue?

He grabbed some towels and took Mason into the shower.

Then it was her turn to shower while he poured the hot chocolate into mugs in the kitchen. He heard the water rushing through the pipes, heard her singing and tried hard not to imagine her in there. He honestly did. But, having seen her in her tight-fitting rash vest and shorts, he knew far too much about her shapely body for his thoughts to keep straying there.

She appeared a few minutes later, her hair wet and curling in waves around her shoulders. Her face was shiny from what he imagined was from one of those face creams in the bathroom. She was wearing a white crop top and white tiered skirt that reached her toes.

He didn't think he'd ever seen anyone so beautiful. It actually hurt his chest. He'd been trying to keep his distance, but he couldn't stop himself from liking her. From wanting her. And he didn't think that he'd feel any different even if she was halfway across the world.

Which didn't bode well for her impending departure.

'Feeling a bit warmer?' she asked as she ambled across the cottage garden to the picnic table and benches where Owen and Mason sat.

'Yes, thanks.' He pushed back from the table and stood, reminding himself of his promise to keep his distance. 'It's probably time we headed off.'

But she frowned, looking at Mason's chocolate moustache, and then at Owen's still half-full cup. 'What's the hurry? Drink up your hot chocolate.'

He gave her a faltering smile, trying to keep the barriers up but failing. 'We need to make a move soon. I've got to get sleepyhead to bed.'

She peered at him, as if looking deep into his soul. He hoped she couldn't see how confused he was. 'Owen, are you okay?'

No. 'Fine, thanks. Why?'

'You seem…off today.'

He pressed his lips together, wondering just how much to say. It wasn't exactly good form for him to admit that he'd been trying to keep his barriers up when she was being so hospitable. He sighed and sat back down. 'Yeah. I'm fine. Honestly. I've just got things on my mind.'

'Such as?'

Luckily his mini-me diverted their attention to two large tents that had been erected on the grass. Mason pointed to them and asked, 'Why have you got tents?'

Carly grinned at his son. 'For the school children to sleep in.'

'Don't they sleep in the house?'

'Not always. The children come to stay for three nights, and for one of them they sleep inside, one of them they have to build their own shelter called a bivouac and for one night they have to set up camp. These two are here for them to learn how to put up a tent. I was going to take them down, but they got very wet in the storm the other night so I'm drying them out.'

Mason looked thoughtful. 'Can I have a look inside?'

'Sure thing.'

Both Owen and Carly said it at the same time.

Great minds.

Mason ran across the grass, disappeared inside the tent and then came back out again, his mouth split in a wide grin. 'It's like a little house. Daddy, can we have a tent?'

Owen glanced over to Carly and gave her a 'kids, hey?' shrug. But she just grinned and mouthed, 'Pushover.'

And here was the thing—he was trying so hard to keep his distance but one smile from her, one word, one look had his heart and, if he was honest, his soul too, barrelling straight towards her again.

He turned his attention to his son. 'Sure thing, buddy. We could go camping—cook sausages on the fire too.'

'And marshmallows?' His son looked at him hopefully.

'Of course. Our own adventure.'

'I like this adventure, Daddy.'

'Me too.' Owen turned and caught Carly looking at him. He smiled and the words tumbled out of his mouth, 'I like this adventure very much.'

Her cheeks bloomed bright red at his words, clearly understanding that they weren't referring to the kayaking. 'Like I said, I'll most likely be selling the kayaks, and I'll offer you a competitive price. In the meantime, feel free to borrow them any time. Same goes for tents. We have a few here and we'll have to sell them off too. Unless the new owner decides to keep the camp as it is. But I can't see that happening.'

'Well, if it makes things easier, I'll definitely buy some stuff from you. Right, Mason? A tent and a kayak?'

'Yes, please.' Then the little boy grabbed his backpack and shuffled back inside the tent.

Which left just the two of them sitting there. Her cheeks still bore glimmers of her blush.

There was so much he wanted to say to her, questions he wanted the answers to… *When will you come back? Is it worth waiting? Are you interested in me, in us? If you came back would you leave again? Do you keep your promises?*

But they all broke his cardinal rule of backing off.

He glanced across the table and caught her gaze.

She smiled.

His body prickled.

He ached to say something important. But instead he turned away from her and looked to the tent. *Coward.*

'Mason? You okay in there?'

'Playing hide and seek with teddy.'

He laughed. There was nothing in the tent to hide behind or under. 'You need anything, just shout.'

'Yes, Dad.'

Carly leaned back in her chair and smiled as she too looked over at the tent. 'He's going to remember this special time you spent with him. You're a great dad, you know that?'

'I wish. But I want to be, so I guess that's half the battle, right?'

Now her laser focus retrained on Owen. 'Must have been hard when his mum left.'

'I was lost, to be honest. We'd tried hard and we'd failed. I watched her pack her things and then leave, and wondered just how long it would be before Mason saw her again. He didn't cope well. We had endless sleepless nights and wails of wanting Mummy. Which made me feel totally inadequate, because there's something about a mother's love, right?'

'I wouldn't know. Although Wendy was lovely.' Carly shrugged sadly.

Damn. How utterly careless of him. 'You'll be a mother one day, and you'll get to lavish those babies with everything you didn't have.'

'Oh, don't worry. I'm going to be the worst kind of mother.' She laughed. 'Helicopter parenting. Spoiling them completely. So much love.'

She really did have so much love to give to the right person. Whoever that might be. Whoever she met on her travels.

She pierced him with her gaze. 'You loved Miranda, right? Once?'

'Of course. She's a remarkable woman and a very talented actress. But she needed to follow her own path.' He paused and looked down at his feet. A sudden sadness filled his chest. 'Just like my mother.'

And now Carly was planning to go too. He needed a way out of this conversation.

He sat up and walked over to the tent. When he crawled in, he found his beautiful boy fast asleep with his teddy bear tucked safely in his arms.

Now what to do? He turned to walk back to Carly but, when he turned round, she was there behind him, so close, in touching distance. Like a worried mother hen. A worried mother. The thought slid into his head, and he banished it immediately. 'He's fast asleep. Completely out for the count. Shame to wake him up, but I really should get him home.'

Her eyes fixed softly on Mason as she whispered, 'Bless. I'll go to the cottage and grab some blankets.'

'Or I should probably wake him up and take him home.'

'Or...don't wake him. You could stay.'

He wasn't sure he understood the subtext of her comment. 'Here?'

'Why not? I've got all the gear. Won't take a minute to grab some sleeping bags and mats.'

He blinked, trying to make sense of her words. 'You'll stay too?'

But she laughed, frowned and kind of blushed all at the same time. 'No! I have a perfectly good bed in the cottage.'

'What if we get scared or attacked by bears?'

She shook her head, eyes full of tease. 'You'll be fine, you big burly man. There are no bears on this island.'

He played along. 'But there are wallabies. Maybe that old guy brought over bears too. Bears you know nothing about.'

'I know every nook and cranny of this island, and I can promise you, there are no bears.'

'That's a shame.'

'Too bad.' She tutted and rolled her eyes. 'Looks like you're staying the night. It's time for that *Boy's Own* adventure you've been promising. I'll bring you both some blankets.'

'And more hot chocolate?'

She gave another eye-roll. 'Okay, and hot chocolate. What an intrepid adventurer you are.'

He laughed, words slipping freely from his lips before he could stop them. 'Hey, I have plenty of ideas to make it more exciting.'

She spluttered, laughed and her eyes twinkled. They were back to being friends, being friendly, and a step closer to that line they'd promised not to cross. 'Okay. I'll bring it all over. Back in a minute.'

In the meantime, he probably needed another dip in the ocean to cool off.

By the time Carly got back to the camping area, the sun had well and truly set. They covered Mason with the blankets and zipped up his tent.

As Owen straightened, something glinting in the water caught his eye. No, not glinting—sparkling. The waves rolling onto the shore were bright with light. 'Look, the water's sparkling. Wow. That's awesome.'

'Bioluminescence. Yes, it happens sometimes. Come and look.' She started to walk towards the shoreline.

But Owen glanced back at the tent and concern rattled his chest. 'What about Mason? What if he wakes up?'

'Seriously, he'll be fine. Hundreds—no, thousands—of children have camped here and been completely safe. We'll only be there...' She pointed to a spot about a hundred metres away.

Reassured, he followed her down to the beach and put a blanket on the sand. They sat down on it, close but not touching.

He stared at the silvery white lights in the ocean wash. 'It's like stars dancing on the waves.'

She looked up at him and smiled. 'Yes. It's exactly that. That's a perfect description.'

And there she was, smiling and perfect herself. 'I've never seen anything so amazing.'

He meant her, of course, but he directed his gaze back to the sea. 'It's beautiful.'

Then he remembered not to remind her about all the fabulous things Rāwhiti Island had going for it. She was clearly finding it hard to leave without remembering all the reasons to stay. Which, he had to admit, was crazy when his whole body was screaming for her touch, for her to stay just long enough for him to kiss her again. But he had to support her plan. That was what friends did. 'How's the sale going?'

'Okay. It's conditional on a builder's report, and a few other things, but all being well we'll be heading off to Auckland in a couple of weeks to sign the paperwork.'

'A couple of weeks? That's quick.' He'd hoped for months. 'When I sold up in Mount Eden it took about twelve weeks for everything to be processed.'

'We're not in a chain, neither is the buyer. Should be smooth running.'

'Do you have to go into the city? You can't sign from here?'

She shook her head. 'Not when lawyers are involved. We have to sign it all in person. Mia and I have decided to have a couple of days' R and R in the city. Then, once the contract is signed, I'm heading off.'

'I'll offer to have Harper, so you can have some child-free fun before you go.' He couldn't believe he was making it so easy for her to leave.

She turned and blinked, surprise filling her expression. 'That's so kind.'

'I know.' He shrugged, feeling so many emotions other than kind. 'I'm selfless to a fault.'

He laughed and lay back on the blanket, looking up at the cloudless night sky, the myriad stars and purple slick of Milky Way.

She lay down next to him. Silence stretched between them. Comfortable, in that he didn't feel a need to fill the gap in conversation. Uncomfortable, because he was painfully aware of her breathing, the rise and fall of her chest and breasts. Her scent.

The fact she was so close, in touching distance but not touching. Painfully not touching.

A couple of weeks? That was all they had left.

No chance for anything to develop even if they both wanted it to.

He closed his eyes and breathed deeply. He was fooling himself by pretending he didn't want to. And the way she looked at him, the way she looked at his son—with such affection and care— made him believe she wanted something too. But maybe they were destined to be just good friends.

Suddenly, he felt the soft brush of her hand against his. For a beat he thought he'd imagined it, or she'd done it by accident, but when her fingers stroked the back of his hand again he knew he'd misjudged.

Just that light touch set his body aflame.

He swallowed, unsure how to outwardly react when internally he was jittery and hot. Jeez, it was the first time he'd been unsure about his next move with a woman. Carly's precarious past, her present vulnerability and the fact she was leaving all gave him pause.

But, man, he ached for her.

He turned on to his side to look at her. To see if what she was doing was intentional. She drew her hand away and turned on her side to face him, her eyes hidden by a floppy lock of hair.

He was so turned on by the simple touch of her skin against his, he could barely form words. *I want you. I want to kiss you. I want to be inside you. Here. Right now. On this magical beach.*

'Hey, Carly,'

'Hey.' She smiled.

He slid a finger under her chin and tilted her head so he could see her face.

And—*oh God, yes*—her moves were intentional. Her eyes were as sparkling as the water. Her mouth was slightly open, her body inching closer.

And, just like the last time, it took just one look…one desperate, sexy, hungry look…and they were in each other's arms.

CHAPTER NINE

LIKE A SPARK to dry tinder, heat crackled through her, searing her nerve endings.

This kiss was as out of control as the first one.

She couldn't stop. Just couldn't stop putting her arms around his neck and drawing him closer. Couldn't stop pressing her lips against his. Tasting him. Feeling the solid weight of him—real, hard, honest. Here.

His throaty groan as her tongue slid against his stoked any remaining embers inside her that hadn't already caught fire.

She pressed against him, fitting herself against his hard body, running her palms over strong shoulders and across his back. She wanted to touch him everywhere.

He laid her back on the blanket and propped himself up on his elbow, his other hand stroking her cheek. 'Carly, we shouldn't be doing this. We agreed.'

She closed her eyes, not ready for a conversation. 'If we dissect it, we'll stop, and I don't want to stop. I don't want to talk. I want to kiss you. I want to touch you. I want to feel. God, I want to just feel, Owen. I want you inside me. So badly.'

His Adam's apple dipped as he swallowed, the expression in his eyes telling her he didn't want this to stop either. 'I want that more than anything, but are you sure?'

She'd been broken before. Completely. Utterly. Wretchedly torn apart. The death of her husband had had her numb one day and then awash with cruel, painful, roiling emotions the next. Rinse and repeat for two whole years. Another year on and she was starting to recover now, a welcome relief from such intense grief.

She'd vowed never to give her heart again, but this…? Surely, this was safe? There was an expiry date. She simply couldn't get emotionally involved, because she was leaving. It would end. They both knew it. So why not enjoy it while it lasted?

'Yes, Owen. I'm sure. We both know the score, right?'

'We do.' His tone was pained but he bent to kiss her again and she closed her eyes, losing herself in the sensations she'd been denying herself from the first moment she'd seen him.

His fingers stroked across her ribs, below her breasts, and she was almost driven crazy with the need for him to slide his hands over her nipples.

She pressed against him, stifling her own groans as her thigh connected with his erection. One slight shift in position and her core pressed against the hard ridge in his shorts. She wanted to rock against him, desperate to feel his hard length inside her.

He kissed a trail from her breasts back to her mouth. 'Carly, you have no idea how much I want this.'

'I think I do.' She moved against his erection teasingly, and giggled.

He inhaled sharply, eyes widening, and groaned. 'You're amazing. I want to see you. All of you.'

He slowly, almost reverently, removed her top. Then he slid the straps of her bra down, kissing trails along each arm. Undid the clasp and dropped her bra to the ground. Then he dipped his head and sucked a nipple in. As she watched the slow, deep suck, she wanted to scream with pleasure but controlled herself so much, her body shook. Or was it trembling out of pure sexual need?

His mouth was hot and his kisses greedy. She felt alive, reckless, wild.

Free.

Yes. Free to be herself. To follow her desires. To take what she wanted. To put away her past… all the good and the bad. To revel in the now.

In this man. Every touch was more fuel to the fire burning inside her. She wanted to beg him to hurry, but also tell him to slow down, so she could revel in every second.

He worked his way up her body, back to her mouth, and she melted into another of his searing kisses until her thoughts were nothing except his taste, his touch, his scent.

Owen Cooper—a surprise and a gift. Her going-away present.

A loud bleeping sound had her pulling away.

What the hell?

Damn. It had been so long since she'd done anything like this. Couldn't she just have had one precious moment with this hot man? Okay...a few precious moments. 'Shoot. What now?'

She peered down at the neon message.

Bush fire. North Bay.

And her heart rattled. 'Oh, hell. Owen, I'm so sorry. I need to go.'

His breathing was rapid, eyes suddenly alert. 'What is it?'

'Bush fire. North Bay. No other details.' Suddenly cold, she sat up, slid her bra straps up her arms, pulled on her top and settled her clothes back in place. Her need for him did not wane. Would she ever stop wanting him? Would ten minutes, ten hours, ten months, ten years away from him douse this burning?

Would a thousand miles? Ten thousand?

He jumped up and ran his palms down his shorts. '*We* need to go. It's a fire…there could be casualties.'

'Okay. Yes. We need to get there ASAP. Everything's so dry, the whole island could go up. What about Mason?' Her heart stalled at the thought of the little boy fast asleep in the tent. A few moments ago, he could have caught them behaving like teenagers. But she was aware he was like most other youngsters and slept heavily.

They'd been safe.

And she felt bereft to have to stop, to peel her hands away from Owen. To have his kisses abruptly terminated.

'I'll see if Mia can have him. I'll call her on the way.' He gave her a sharp nod, all business. 'I'll just go wake him up. What about more help?'

'We've got it covered…unless it gets too big. Then we radio for help from the mainland. The coastguard brings the other volunteer firefighters round from other parts of the island, and I have my gear and the jet-ski, so I'll head straight over now. There's a depot down at the yacht club with emergency equipment. Wiremu's son, Nikau, will bring over the smoke chaser. I'll meet you there. North Bay.'

'And then?' His hand snaked around her waist, drawing her closer to that toned chest.

She inhaled his scent, pressed a kiss to his throat then stepped away. 'I think the universe is telling us this is not going to happen.'

He nodded again and she couldn't read him. Was he relieved they'd been interrupted or as frustrated as she was? Every time they moved forward, they took more than a few steps back.

And he was all closed down again, seemingly in agreement that it wasn't going to happen again.

No matter how much she ached for it.

Having quickly dropped Mason off at Mia's, Owen steered into the bay and secured his own boat up against the jetty, then ran towards the smoke and flames. Judging by the number of boats anchored in North Bay, the whole island had come to fight the fire. Two locals had fire hoses attached to their jet-skis, pointing plumes of water towards the bushes on the west side of the bay. A helicopter hovered overhead, dumping a huge bucket of water over the trees towards the east.

His heart had barely recovered from the intensity of their passion, then the dousing of it. Now, trying to find Carly in the chaos of the scene, he wondered at the wisdom of snatching kisses like that when she was not going to be around in a couple of weeks.

He shoved those thoughts to the back of his mind.

We both know the score.

He did. They hadn't committed to anything serious, just a few kisses. He could walk away any time and still keep his heart intact.

Smoke filled the air, flames flickered high in the bush and the smell of burning tinged every inhale. But the sounds surprised him more than anything. He hadn't expected fire crackle to be so loud.

He dashed over to a familiar face who was pulling out a hose reel attached to a high-pressure pump on a quad bike. The Rāwhiti Island smoke chaser. 'Nikau, are you okay?'

The young man nodded. 'Sure.'

'Any injured?'

'Not so far.'

'Thank God.' But Owen knew that it was probably only a matter of time before his skills would be needed. He didn't want to think about the kind of injuries people could sustain in a bush fire, but was as prepared as he could be. He dropped his doctor's bag and helped unroll the hose reel. 'Have you seen Carly?'

'She was over there, last time I looked.' Nikau pointed towards a group of firefighters in helmets and mustard-yellow gear heaving a pulsing water hose in the direction of the thickest smoke. 'Thanks for the help, Doc. I'm good to go.'

Owen ran to the huddle of firefighters and there…in the middle of the line of these valiant, volunteer first responders…was the woman he'd had so much respect for. And now it skyrocketed.

'Carly!'

She turned at the sound of her name, her eyes seeking him out, her posture softening as she found him. She gave him a small smile. 'You made it.'

'Yes. Any one hurt? What's on fire? Just bush or houses too?'

'It's closing in on Anahera's home. If we can get this water closer, we can hopefully stop it before it spreads further.'

'On three,' one of the firefighters at the front of the line called out. 'One. Two. Three!'

As they started to run towards the fire, Owen's heart lurched. 'Be careful.'

Please, be careful.

Carly turned back to look at him. For one tiny second their eyes locked and he tried to convey to her, in that briefest of looks, all the jumble of things in his chest. He wished her to be safe. He wished… *Hell*, he just wished she'd come back to him.

Then she was gone, disappearing into the trees,

the darkness and the swirl of smoke that felt as if it had curled into his chest and wrapped tightly around his heart.

'Help! Help us, please!' Over on his left, two people staggered out of the smoking bush, their faces covered in black streaks, hands covering their mouths as they coughed and struggled for air.

Pushing his fears for Carly's safety away, he ran to help the casualties—Anahera and her husband—and hooked them up to the portable oxygen, assessing for smoke inhalation, burns and shock. When they were able to answer, he asked, 'How close is the fire to your home?'

Anahera shook her head and sighed. 'It was closing in on the barn when we left. We hosed everything down and, luckily, we'd just finished pruning and thinning the bigger trees. We just have to hope they can stop it in time.'

Owen Cooper wasn't a praying man but right then and there he sent up a message to whoever would listen that Anahera's house would be saved, and that Carly would come out of this unhurt.

His receptionist put a warm hand over his. 'Are you thinking twice about having moved here, Doc?'

'Well, there's certainly never a dull moment on

Rāwhiti, is there?' He peered towards the bush, looking for Carly.

Anahera gave a sad, throaty huff as she followed his gaze. 'That's why we love it.'

Two firefighters staggered out of the bush and he ran to assist them, dressing their minor burns and giving them water.

No Carly.

Where was she?

How was she?

Two more people were brought to him, people with smoke inhalation, cuts and grazes. Then more—a potentially torn retina from a falling branch, a panic attack, more burns...

And through it all he kept half an eye out for Carly. His heart wouldn't stop pounding against his ribcage, as his attention was continually being pulled back to that little path into the dense trees, desperately searching for her to walk out.

And he realised the agony she must have endured, waiting for her husband to come home. The torment and pain she'd lived through, the slow realisation he wasn't coming back. The final acceptance that he was dead. How had she lived through that to become the amazing woman she was now? How had she not let that taint everything?

And why had she chosen him, Owen Cooper, to be the one she now bestowed with sexy-sweet kisses? The one to bring her back to life after her years in grief?

He didn't have any answers, just a heart full of panic, pain and hope.

It was two hours before she returned, covered in soot and sweating from the heat and the restricting uniform. She bent forward to catch her breath and he stroked her back as she coughed and cleared her throat. He was beyond glad to see her and yet…he couldn't name the emotion that sat heavily in his chest. Frustration? Helplessness? Anger? He wanted to shake her for scaring him so much. He wanted to wrap her in his arms and kiss her. He wanted to hold her and not let her go.

Then, finally, yes…he admitted to himself that he wanted her to stay. But that was a futile dream.

The other firefighters were close, a team working and resting together. Even if he knew what he was feeling, he wasn't going to express it in front of these people.

He handed her a water bottle. 'Drink.'

She took it and gulped down half its contents. Then she hauled in a deep breath, a frown forming as she looked at him, searching his face. 'You okay?'

He chose not to answer, not trusting himself

to be able to hold every emotion in. 'How's Ana-hera's house?'

'We got to it just in time. It's okay. The barn's gone. The trees around her property are badly singed. It was a very close call.'

'You could have been killed in there.'

It was only now that he recognised the emotion: desperation. The same root as the frantic need to kiss her, and now, the panic about her safety. He'd never felt this—not when his mother had left, not when Miranda had filed for divorce—a desperate ache for another person.

But it was a two-sided coin. An insatiable need and an absolute threat to his equilibrium.

She glanced at him, still frowning. 'But I wasn't killed, Owen. I'm fine. I know my limitations. I know when to go in and when to stand down. I stick to all the health and safety rules.'

'I... I...' He paced back and forth, trying to douse the other emotions rushing through him—fear, anger, want, need—and failing. When it came to Carly, it was all or nothing.

All.

He lowered his voice. 'I thought I was going to lose you.'

'You can't get rid of me that easily.' She grinned and winked. The wink was for fun, for the observers and volunteers all watching this interaction. But the smile was for him. 'But thank you for caring.'

'Carly?' Nikau called over, giving her the thumbs-up. 'Just had confirmation from the helicopter that it's all out. They'll do some regular flyovers overnight to check and the Blue Team will stay on and keep watch. You get off home.'

'Thank God.' She sighed and smiled, exhaustion bruising below her eyes. Then she turned back to Owen. 'You go get some sleep too.'

'Sure.' He nodded, fighting the urge to pick her up and take her back to his place.

Thank you for caring?

His heart had almost hammered its way out of his chest, which should have been a warning that he was getting too involved, but he didn't want to listen. He knew he was getting involved…but he was on a collision course he couldn't stop. The rush was addictive. The *utter desperation* of their kisses, the frantic energy, made him feel the most alive he'd ever been. He couldn't walk away. He had a matter of weeks to sink into it. The rest of his life to remember it.

He didn't want to sleep. He wanted to sear her image on his brain. Her beautiful face streaked with soot, her eyes alive with adrenalin. And her kisses. Her taste.

Why would a man sleep when he could relive that over and over?

CHAPTER TEN

JUST HOW FAR would they have gone if the fire alarm hadn't gone off? A question Carly pondered all night, and again the next morning, as she hosed down the kayaks after her last lesson.

All the way? Some of the way?

She had to tried to forget it, but she couldn't. He was all she could think about. The way he'd looked at her with such desire on the beach, the kiss, then the panic she'd felt resonate off him at the fire. Panic about her safety. Care for her.

Such intensity made her giddy. And she craved it, relished it.

Her last retort about him caring had been offhand and probably rude, but it was the only way she'd been able to shake the need to slide into his arms again, especially in front of all the people who knew her and had known her husband and in-laws.

After Raff, was it wrong of her to want another man? She didn't think so. Not after all this time. She didn't feel guilty about being attracted to Owen. Raff was gone and she'd grieved him—so much. Of course, she still missed him. His loss was a piece of her heart that would never be filled. He'd given her roots she'd so badly needed and a home she'd never had before. A place to be. A family.

But that was all gone now, and she knew he'd want her to be happy. She just wasn't sure what steps she needed to take to make it happen.

She'd thought that travel would help her find her way, but now there was Owen. He wasn't a Raff replacement. No one could ever be that. Raff had been amazing. But there were other men, amazing in different ways to her husband.

Owen.

His expression as she'd come out of the bush was seared onto her brain. He cared. Really cared.

And she liked him too.

But, what now?

Confused, exhausted from the late night and overly emotional, she took photos of each of the kayaks and the optimist boats and then went inside to her laptop to upload them to the marketplace website. This bit was hard—selling off the camp things, drawing that line under her old life—but it was necessary. As necessary as following through on her promise to see the world and give herself some well-needed space from this island, from the pain that reared every now and then. Less intense, and less frequent, but it was still there. And space, too, from Owen. Every moment spent with him was fuzzing her head. She needed fresh perspective and she wouldn't get that by staying here.

So she did what she'd been planning to do for a long time but had kept putting off. After she'd clicked 'enter', she inhaled deeply and blew out slowly. It was actually happening.

Chase it, girl. You only have one life.

Raff used to say that to her about so many opportunities she'd almost turned down because she hadn't felt good enough, or worthy or had felt that she might fail. Coming from the background she did, she'd developed an outward veneer of capability and independence, but inside she was a mass of insecurity and self-doubt. What if she wasn't good enough? What if she failed? What if she didn't fit in?

Basically, what if she was rejected or abandoned all over again?

Knowing this about herself, though, didn't mean she could always rise above it. It just meant she'd learnt to cover her self-doubts well. But Raff had been a good teacher and had been amazing for her self-esteem. Hell, the man had chosen her, had married her. If his death had taught her anything, it was that she needed to grab every opportunity with both hands.

The sound of a boat engine had her glancing out of the window.

Owen.

Her heart jittered as she thought of him last night, grimy and smoky, giving first aid to all those people. She'd put out a fire, but he'd made sure everyone had stayed safe. They were a great team.

And now he was running down the jetty.

Her heart rate doubled. What the hell had happened? The fire…had it flared into life again? No. She'd have been alerted. And where was his mini-me shadow? Where was his son?

Panic gripped her chest as she ran across the grass and met him at the playground. 'What's the matter? What's happened? Is everything okay?'

'Yes. And no. Everything's not okay. Not for me. I just wanted…' His breath was ragged and jumpy, his eyes telling her that the only emergency was his need to be here with her. 'I just wanted you, Carly.'

He wanted her, still.

'God, Owen.' She put her hand on his chest and felt the rapid fire of his heart. The solid muscle. His heat. Relief shimmied through her, along with excitement at his words. 'I thought there was a crisis.'

'There is. I can't sleep. I can't do anything. I just want this…' He pulled her to him the way he had last night at the beach, his arms strong and steady as they circled her waist. His fresh shower scent filled the air. 'I want you, Carly.'

Her body instantly responded to his touch the way it had last night. The embers deep inside her burst back into flames. She curled into his embrace. 'Yes.'

It was the only answer.

Then there were no more words as he tilted his mouth to hers and kissed her so achingly slowly, and with such need and care, that her insides felt as if they were melting into liquid. This kiss was so different from the others. It was a gift so beautiful, so wonderful, she felt herself drifting in sensation after sensation. His mouth, his tongue. His touch.

Finally, he released her, smiling as she stepped back to catch her breath, and what she saw in his eyes made her blush. 'Um…where's Mason?'

His smile grew more sexy. 'Still at Mia's. They had a broken night, so she's hoping they'll sleep late. We've got a few hours.'

Carly swallowed, her mouth suddenly wet and dry at the same time as she anticipated their next move. 'So, no interruptions?'

'Nothing but you and me and this…' He slipped his hands under her knees and swung her up into his arms.

Whoa. He was playful too. Could she like him

any more? She giggled, crying out, 'What the hell do you think you're doing, Dr Cooper?'

He took a step forward. 'What I wanted to do last night. What I've wanted to do since the moment I set eyes on you, fifty metres from here. Your hair was a tangle and your face all screwed up in anger as you shouted at me. I wanted you that very second.'

Oh, God. She was lost.

He made short work of the distance to the house and up the stairs to her bedroom. He laid her down on the coverlet and kissed her again, mussing her thoughts and awakening every cell in her body.

As she shifted underneath him, she put her hand on his arm. Time to be honest, even if it meant putting an end to this right now. 'Listen, Owen. I need you to know that I've bought a plane ticket. One way to London, with stopovers all the way. I'm actually doing it. In two weeks' time.'

'Okay.' The light in his eyes dimmed for a second as he took in her words before it flickered back to life again. He pressed his lips to her throat, making her squirm. 'All the more reason for us to make the most of this time, then.'

She sighed against him. 'I hoped you'd say that.'

He stripped her top off and unclipped her bra.

Then he paused, looking at her with something akin to greedy adoration. His fingers stroked around her nipple, teasing. 'I know this is probably crazy, and stupid, and might mess everything up. But I don't care. I can't stop thinking about you. I can't stop wanting you.' His mouth captured hers again.

Breathless, she panted out, 'All I want…is this moment.'

'I'm hoping it'll last longer than a moment.' He guffawed as he lowered his head and took her nipple into his mouth. Hot shivers of lust rippled through her, making her writhe against him. She pulled his head up and kissed him again, dragging off his T-shirt and smoothing her hands across his chest.

As she did so, she glanced across the room, catching a glimpse of the engraved kauri wood jewellery box Raff had made for her as a wedding gift. The box in which she kept her wedding ring. Her heart gave an involuntary shudder. She closed her eyes.

Owen must have sensed her hesitation. He pulled back to look at her and stroked her cheek. 'Hey. Are you okay?'

She blinked and looked up into his handsome face. Was she okay? She was in bed with a man who wasn't her husband. With a man who made her feel the most sexy she'd felt for years. Who lifted her heart. Who made her laugh. Who made her believe in herself and what she could achieve. Who listened. Who she trusted with her heart— totally. She wanted this. She wanted him.

'Yes, Owen. I am very okay.'

'You know we can stop any time. We can just talk. We can do whatever you want.'

Her heart flooded with warmth and she smiled, because how could she not? He was so caring and considerate, and an amazing kisser. She only hoped he was as good at sex. Because that was where she was heading right now. 'Is that a promise?'

He nuzzled against her. 'Absolutely.'

'Good. I want you to kiss me.'

He leaned in and kissed her again. It started as a repeat of the slow-build kiss from earlier, but before long it was frantic and so damned hot, every nerve ending was crying out for his touch. She arched against him, trying to fit her body tight against his. To feel all of him along all of her.

He grabbed her butt cheek and squeezed playfully. 'These short shorts drive me absolutely crazy. Every time you wear them I imagine what's underneath.'

'This is my work wear.' She chuckled as she ran her fingers suggestively around the waistband of her shorts. 'You like a woman in uniform?'

His eyes widened as he watched her play with the denim. 'To be honest, I think I'm going to prefer you with no uniform. No clothes at all.'

'Be my guest.' She raised her hips and wriggled as he unzipped her shorts and drew them down her legs, then her panties. He sucked in a breath as he looked at her. 'Jeez, Carly, you are so damned beautiful.'

And she felt it. She felt beautiful for the first time in years. Felt wanted, needed. Felt important to someone. To Owen. This fine, sexy man. The heat in his eyes almost seared her skin. She would have blushed had she not felt deep-down sexy too. Instead, she felt emboldened. Renewed. Alive again.

She slid her hand down his chest, skimming over his flat belly to that delicious line of dark hair arrowing to his erection. She palmed his hardness and laughed as he groaned into her ear. Then she unzipped his fly and took him in her hand. He was so hard. So big.

She stroked him. He groaned again and arched against her. 'God, that feels good.'

'I want you inside me,' she whispered against his throat. He smelt so good, tasted so fine. Her body pulsed with desire. She didn't think she could wait...

'In time. Too soon.' He pulled away, put his hand over hers and stopped her stroking.

She growled and pretended to pout. 'You said you'd do whatever I wanted. I want you inside me.'

'Oh? Demanding now, hey?' He kissed down her breasts, across her belly and then lower. 'I will do exactly what you want. But *when* I want.'

His eyes fired tease, fun and heat, and then he parted her thighs and dipped his head to her core.

When his mouth made contact with the little bundle of nerve-endings, she laid her head back on the pillow, unable to stop the whimper coming from her throat.

She lost herself in the dizzying magic of his tongue, arching against him as he slid a finger inside her, then another. She felt herself clench around him, her thoughts and emotions spiralling into a blur of touch and sensation...his mouth... his tongue...his fingers giving her so much pleasure, her body pulsed and shook.

How long had it been since she'd been touched like this?

Then she didn't think at all. She rocked against him as her orgasm broke, racking her body in ripple after ripple of mind-warping sensations.

He kissed back up her body and she sat up, reaching for him. 'Wow. That was something else.'

'No, you are.' He cupped her face, pushing her hair back. 'You look sublime, Carly. Like something I've dreamed up. Shimmering. Bloody magical.'

Her chest contracted at his words. She'd wanted sex but hadn't expected the flood of emotions that came with it, emotions for this man. She'd never imagined this could happen again, that she'd feel these things—not just sexy, but wanted and frantic with desire.

One orgasm wasn't enough. She wrapped her legs around his thighs, drawing him closer and closer, wiggling underneath him so his erection was at her entrance, almost wild with desire. 'I need you, Owen. I need you inside me.'

'No hurry.' His gaze caught onto hers and held, serious yet fun, reverential yet playful. He leaned over the side of the bed, produced a condom from his shorts pocket and was sheathed and back in position in no time.

'So much hurry.' She rubbed the heart of her against his erection. 'Please.'

'Well, I suppose so. I did say I'd do anything you want.' He shrugged and laughed, as if sex with her would be no big deal. But his eyes told her a completely different story; he was alight with need for her.

'Don't you dare stop.' She licked up his neck and he gasped, 'I wouldn't dare.'

Then he moved his hips and entered her on a

thick, slick thrust. He gasped again. 'Oh. Wow. You're so ready for me.'

She breathed through the pleasure-pain point—it had been a few years, after all—then sighed as her body relaxed to let him in.

'I... I don't even know what to say. That feels so good. *You* feel so good.' She found his mouth and kissed him again.

'You are amazing.' He thrust again, then withdrew almost wholly, then slid inside her again.

'Oh, God. Please, never stop. Never...stop.' There was heat everywhere, low down in her core, in her belly and bright white heat in her chest. She was all aglow for him.

She lifted her face to watch him and their eyes locked. Gone was the playfulness and the fun, replaced by someone intent, driven and so damned sexy.

And suddenly it wasn't enough. She wanted harder and faster. She wanted all of him. She clawed at his hair and his skin, fingers raking down his back.

He groaned and changed his rhythm, and she matched it, forcing him to thrust deeper and faster and harder. To fill her completely. And, as she finally lost all control, his name was on her lips over and over and over.

But when he growled her name on a loud sigh she completely broke open, torn apart with need and want and an earth-shattering release. She clung to him, pressing against him, skin to skin, body to body, chest to chest as she rode their climax. Gripping him.

Would she ever have enough of him?

Two weeks. The plans were made. The ticket was bought. There were just signatures to be given. She would be free. Mia and Harper would be financially secure.

But what of Carly? What of her plans? Would she be able to relax completely into her new adventure, meeting new people, visiting new places, experiencing the world and growing? Or would she be forever looking back at Rāwhiti Island for the man she'd lost and the man she'd just found?

Oh, Owen. Why did I find you now?

It was the worst timing ever. She'd spent her life craving a family—her family—stumbling from one to another, being rejected or neglected. Then the one time she'd finally come home, the foundations had been ripped away.

And now…now another little unit was pulling her closer. But what if…? What if she allowed herself to fall into it and it was all ripped away again?

What then of Carly Edwards? She wouldn't be able to cope if she lost them too.

It was better for her to leave. Not to forge bonds.

But it was so hard.

Why did it have to be so hard?

In the silence that followed Owen closed his eyes and took some deep, steadying breaths. His heart hammered at the exertion, but more…it hammered because of the emotions swirling through him. Emotions he didn't want to name. Hell, he didn't know if there was a single name for *adoration, yearning desperation, delight, release…*

All quickly followed by alarm that gripped his chest like a vice. Because it didn't matter how much he told himself this was just sex, that this was just temporary, this was just a moment… her moment. He couldn't imagine not wanting it again, on repeat for ever.

He held her tight against him as her body relaxed after her orgasm. Her fingers stroked down his back and her head nestled against his throat.

Two weeks.

Two weeks and then nothing. No more of this. No more snatched kisses. No more pretending this wasn't something when it was plain to him now that it was…everything.

He'd promised himself he could deal with it. But how could he deal with losing Carly?

How had he let himself fall so hard for her when she was yet another woman leaving his life?

How could he be so cavalier with his heart?

He suddenly couldn't get his breath. He needed air. He gently slid out and away from her, trying to make some space, but realising it didn't matter how far away from her he was. The attachment wasn't geographical, it was inside him.

She smiled lazily and stroked his thigh. 'You rushing off?'

Her expression told him she didn't want him to.

'Not at all. Just getting comfortable,' he lied. Well, he hadn't been about to leave, just give himself some breathing space.

The exact words she'd used about her upcoming trip. And he got it now. The emotions rolling through him threatened his sense and his equilibrium. If every thought was tinged with her, then how could he be objective about anything? If every thought she had was connected to this island and to her past, then how could she be objective about her future?

She had to leave to make sense of everything.

And he had to stay to give his son the stable home and security he deserved.

He probably should have been honest and explained. He should have admitted he needed space to breathe. But, instead, Owen leaned up on his elbow and breathed her in, grasping every moment they had left. Selfish. Greedy. Reckless.

The afternoon sun caught the gold and red strands of her hair splayed out on the white pillow. She was breathtakingly gorgeous as her expression turned from concern to satisfaction.

She blinked up at him, her eyes searching his face, and he wondered if he imagined something sad there for a moment. But then she smiled and rubbed her head against his arm. 'That was amazing, Owen.'

'It was.' He ran a finger down her cheek, wondering if she could feel the panic in his touch.

But she just kept on smiling. 'Thank you.'

'For what?'

'For showing me that I can be me again. That I'm not just a widow. That I'm capable of feeling.' Her eyes filled with tears and his throat closed over. He pulled her into his arms and hugged her close.

'You are so much more. You're…a miracle.' And, as she'd gone there, he followed. 'I wasn't sure if you were going to be okay with it—you know, after Raff.'

Her chest rose as she inhaled. Then she swallowed. 'I…um… I didn't know either. But I was okay with it. I am.'

'He sounds like he was a great guy.'

'He was.' She put her hand on his chest and edged backwards, more to look at him, he thought, than to make space between them. 'But we shouldn't be talking about him.'

'Why not?'

She frowned. 'I thought it might upset you.'

'God, Carly, no. Not at all. You have a past, so do I. We all have… I don't want to call it baggage, because your life with Raff is not something that dragged you down, it clearly gave you joy…' He dug deep for the right words, because he didn't want Mason to be thought of as baggage either. 'We all have *experiences* that we've had to live through. But I want to know you better, and that means we have to be open. I don't want you to edit what you say or think just to make me feel better about something. Raff was the most important person in your life. Please don't censor your thoughts or words about him.'

Her eyebrows rose as she looked at him and the tears welled again as she cupped his cheek. 'You're a remarkable man, Owen.'

'Not really. I lived with a woman who tried to be something she wasn't. And that just ended in disaster. I don't want you to feel you can't say what you think or feel around me.' He shrugged. 'Maybe I'm just being selfish and lazy, because I don't want to have to guess where your head is at.'

'You're a single dad who wants the best for his kid and a doctor who serves the island, Owen. There is nothing selfish or lazy about you.'

'I'm just greedy to know more about you, really. If ever you want to talk about Raff, or what happened or anything at all, I'm here.'

She slid out of his arms and propped herself up against the pillows. She sat for a few moments, staring into space, deep in thought, and he didn't want to push her, so he sat in the silence and waited.

Eventually she turned to him and he sensed she didn't want to be touched as she said, 'I waited for him. And waited. And prayed. I don't even know who to. The skies? The water? Anyone who'd listen…yes, God, if there is one. Anyone. Prayed for him to come back to me. I'd wake up thinking it was all a dream, and then the cold, black reality would come crashing in. And that's how it was for over a week until they finally gave up looking.'

A thick weight pressed on his chest. 'I thought I hurt when my mum left, and I prayed for her to come home, but this is on another level altogether. I can't imagine the pain you lived through.'

She shook her head. 'You don't live. You barely survive. Thank God for the island people, they were so lovely. They sent out search parties, held vigils, filled my freezer with food I couldn't stomach. I couldn't eat. Didn't sleep. We were in a sort of limbo for days. I couldn't make sense of any of it. Their disappearance made no sense to me. Raff's family lived on the water. They knew it so well.'

Her expression crumpled into anguish. 'Then

they found Raff's dad's body off one of the neighbouring islands. So we knew then, for sure. Not what had happened, but that they weren't coming back. I was numb. I was raging. I was desperate. I was scared. I was…so many things.' She wrapped her arms round her knees and hugged them close to her chest. 'I was alone. Again.'

He put his hand on her shoulder and she shuffled close and leant her head on his arm. He wanted to tell her that she didn't have to feel alone again. Ever. But he sensed it wasn't the right time, or maybe even the right thing to say, because she was choosing to travel solo. She needed her alone adventure.

But he imagined her broken and raging, and then stumbling numbly through each day. How hard she must have prayed and searched. How hard she'd worked to recover. And he had nothing but admiration for the woman she'd become, despite everything she'd been through.

Maybe it was more than admiration. More than sexual attraction. More than care…so much more.

Maybe… The pressing weight on his chest intensified. The panic returned. He couldn't love her. No, that wasn't where he was with this. But he held her in…high esteem. Because love would be too devastating, too much to feel for someone who was leaving.

He would not allow that emotion to creep in.

He just wouldn't. He'd loved and lost too many times now to willingly walk right into that again.

After a few minutes, she took a deep breath and sighed, then blinked up at him and smiled. 'So, what are your plans for the rest of the day?'

What he wanted was to stay here and make love to her again, but if he was going to keep his heart intact he needed to leave, and soon. 'I'll go collect Mason, then we've got a day of decorating. We've moved on to the outside now. God, it all sounds so small and mundane compared to your big adventure.' But he wouldn't change it for the world. Mason was where his focus needed to be.

'Not at all. You're making a life for you and your son. It's beautiful.' She slid her palms down the crisp white sheets. 'I've got to list a load of things for sale.'

'Ugh. I've been there when we downsized our house in the city. Do you need a hand?' And, yes, it appeared he was looking for excuses to stay just a little longer. Like an addict craving the one thing he shouldn't have.

She smiled, oblivious to the turmoil in his chest. 'Thanks, but no. Mia's going to come over later with Harper for a sleepover. We're going to go through everything that needs to be sold, donated or thrown away.'

'You missed out *kept*. If you have anything you

want stored, I can look after it for you. The shed is now clean and tidy.'

'It's fine. Thank you. When it comes down to it, I don't have much. Raff and I met when we were travelling and only had the bags on our backs. We weren't married long enough to accumulate too many things. Mia's going to look after my precious stuff.' Her eyes darted towards a small wooden box on the dressing table. It was a beautiful hand-carved thing with inlaid paua shell on the lid. He guessed either the box or the contents were important to her.

'Because you don't know when you'll be back to collect it.'

She pressed her lips together then nodded slowly. 'Exactly that.'

And there, right there, was the moment he should have left. But instead he pulled her to him, nuzzling her hair, on a trajectory he seemingly had no control over. 'So… I have maybe ten more minutes before I have to collect Mason. You want a hand sorting anything out?'

She laughed and straddled his lap, her beautiful breasts pressing against his chest. 'You can definitely sort me out, Owen Cooper.'

Then she kissed him again and, with that one single act, all his promises to keep his heart intact fell away.

CHAPTER ELEVEN

THEY WERE PAINTING the front of the house when Carly arrived the next afternoon. As she drove down the gravel driveway, she watched them work, man and boy side by side. Owen was dressed in an old paint-splattered T-shirt and denim cut-offs. Mason wore a white *Mr Happy* T-shirt and yellow shorts.

Owen said something to his son that she couldn't hear, but the boy looked up, beamed at his dad and chuckled. Then Owen put down his paint brush, picked Mason up and threw him over his shoulder. He jogged in a circle, with the child screaming, giggling and waving his paint brush in the air, then put him down.

Most people would have been worried about the splashes of white paint on the ground. But not Owen. He just cared about making his son happy.

Her heart constricted. Yesterday had been intense and wonderful, a surprise and a gift. But they hadn't discussed what happened now. Were they neighbours with benefits? Friends? Temporary lovers?

What, exactly?

Feeling a little unsure about it all, she climbed out of the truck and pasted on a smile. 'Hi, guys!'

'Hi, Carly.' Grinning, Mason waved his paint brush again while Owen's slow grin was almost too lazy and sexy for words. She took in the muscled arms that had held her tight as he'd entered her, the mouth that had given her so much pleasure, and her body hummed for more. So, part of her question was answered. They were two single people who'd had consensual sex and they both wanted to do it again. Why put more of a label on it than that?

'Where do you want me to put this?' Trying to rein in her libido, she pointed to the bright orange double kayak strapped to the flat bed of her truck. 'I saved the best one for you two. The rest are up on the marketplace website. Four have sold already.'

'It's a beauty.' Owen sauntered over, looking simply delicious as he wiped his hands on a towel. 'Let's put it in the shed. Mason, are you okay waiting here for a few minutes while I help Carly?'

The boy nodded, serious again and concentrating on his work. 'Sure, Dad.'

'Don't go anywhere. Just paint that corner. You're doing a great job, mate.'

Carly's heart jittered. It was all well and good for her to want sex again, but did he? Had he had second thoughts? Did he regret what they'd done?

But as soon as they'd put the kayak on the ground he was in front of her, toying with a curl of her hair, running it through his fingers, his eyes searching her face. 'Hey, you.'

'Hey, you.' Her heart hammered and her body tugged towards him as she played with the hem of his T-shirt.

'Come here.' He wrapped an arm round her waist and dragged her closer, kissing her deeply, and she felt exactly how much he wanted her.

But she reluctantly pulled away, her hand on his chest. His heart beat hard and fast like hers. 'What about Mason?'

'True.' Owen grimaced and turned to look at the open doorway. 'He's very quiet.'

'Is that a good thing? Or bad?'

'You can never tell with kids. But usually bad.' Smiling, he slipped his hand into hers and squeezed. Then he let go and strode out into the sunshine. Mason was still in the same place, painting the corner, his tongue jutting out in concentration just like his father's had.

Her heart swooped. 'Good job, Mason. You're an expert painter.'

'Thank you, Carly.' He beamed up at her. 'Can we go kayaking now?'

She caught Owen's eye and raised her eyebrows in question. He shook his head. 'Not today, champ. It's getting late, and it's dinner time soon.'

A cue to leave. But her feet seemed reluctant to turn her round and walk her back to the truck. She forced out a lame, 'I'll leave you to it, then.'

Owen met her eyes and smiled secretively. 'You want to stay for dinner? It's nothing special, just sausages and a bit of salad and bread.'

'Man food,' Mason said, and showed her his arm muscles.

'Is that what Daddy calls sausages? Well, I like them too. So, it's also girl food.' She showed him her guns and Mason ran over to squeeze them. 'Wow. You're strong.'

She wished she was, she really did. Was she strong enough to go on her trip? To leave this new friendship, leave everything she knew? She sighed. 'Okay, I'll stay for dinner. But only because you're serving my favourite girl food, and only on the condition that I do the washing up.'

It was almost a rerun of the first time she'd stayed for dinner…partly because Mason insisted on marshmallows by the fire again, and partly because they were both so welcoming. Mason tripped off tales about kindy and his friends and more about Wallace the weka.

Carly laughed at the bird's apparent antics. 'And is she still waking you up every morning?'

'*He* hasn't been able to break down our hardy defences so far.' Owen's expression was a mixture of humour, surprise and censure. Clearly, he hadn't confessed the bird gender confusion to his son.

'It's only a matter of time before she…er…he does.' She giggled at their shared joke.

Shared. Her throat felt scratchy at the thought of leaving these people she'd become so fond of.

'Right. I'll go clear up.' She washed the dishes in the newly decorated kitchen while Owen put Mason to bed. He'd done a great job of sprucing up the place and had even added some soft furnishings that made the house more homely. That was surprising for a guy. She could hear him reading a bedtime story as she flicked the switch for the kettle.

This was all feeling very cosy. He'd called it mundane and small, but wasn't giving a child a secure and stable upbringing one of the most amazing things a parent could do? Even though Mason's mum wasn't around, he had the safety and love of his father. It was home. It was a family—something she'd had a brief taste of and had loved.

But now… No, she couldn't move into this

heart space. She had to create something for herself.

There was no denying she ached to stay here just a little longer, but was that just because she was wobbling about her plans? About stepping into the unknown?

She was reaching to put the plates in a high cupboard when she felt a kiss on her neck, arms circling her waist. A hard erection pressed against her bottom. She whirled round and caught Owen's mouth in a searing kiss.

'You smell so good,' she managed as she pulled away, her body straining for his touch all over.

He laughed. 'Mason's bath bubbles?'

'No. Something else. Something that makes me...'

He held her arms by her sides as he looked at her, his eyes misted and heat shimmering there. 'Horny?'

She giggled. 'Yes.'

'You could stay.'

What? A pause. Maybe he read the confusion on her face because he followed it up with a quick, 'The night, I mean.'

'Oh. No. I shouldn't.' For a moment she'd thought he was asking something else. But...no. He knew her plans.

His fingers tiptoed to the back of her neck and

he stroked the sensitive skin there. 'Do you have to be back at the camp tonight?'

'Well...no.' She inhaled a stuttering breath as his fingers trailed down her back. *God*, that felt good. 'The school teachers are very capable and experienced, and they know how to contact me in an emergency. I have my bleeper.'

'Which I hope remains silent.' He lifted her hair and kissed her neck, making her shudder in delight.

Her determination to leave melted away. Just one touch and she was his. 'I can stay a while, but perhaps it'll be better if I don't sleep over.'

'Stay, Carly.' He kissed down her spine and across her shoulder. 'I want to wake up with you.'

Oh, what a lovely idea. What a wonderfully amazing idea. But no. She turned and captured his mouth in a kiss. She would stay a while. She would leave in the middle of the night. No need for any concerns. No need for questions.

No damage to anyone. Just a lot of fun...while it lasted.

Tap. Tap. Tap.
    Tap. Tap. Tap.
    Tap. Tap. Tap.
    What the hell...?
Someone was doing Morse Code in Carly's bedroom. She opened an eye and took in the

dark drapes, the fingers of yellow light streaming through the gaps. Took in the sleeping body next to her with his arm slung casually over her hip. The unfamiliar shapes of furniture she hadn't chosen.

No. Not *her* bedroom.

She jerked upright. *Hell.* After an amazing night of lovemaking, she'd fallen asleep in his arms and now it was morning.

'Shoo. Get out. Get out!' she whispered at the weka that was tapping the wooden floor.

'Again? How the hell did he get in?' A bleary-eyed Owen rose up next to her. 'What time is it?'

Carly glanced at the clock over on Owen's bedside table. *Oh, no. Oh, no. Oh, no.* 'It's seven-seventeen.'

A string of curse words rose inside her and she put her hand to her mouth to hold them back.

'What?' Owen bounded out of bed. 'Damn it. I am so late.'

Suddenly aware of her nakedness, and also suddenly shy, she grabbed the top sheet and wrapped it round her—as if he hadn't just spent hours caressing and kissing every inch of her—while she scrambled from the bed to find her clothes, keeping her voice a hoarse whisper. 'I have never slept in in my life. I wake at six every morning. I don't need an alarm clock.'

'Me neither, I usually have Mason to wake me

at way too early o'clock and, well, I'd thought I'd got rid of Wallace.' He quietly shooed the bird out of the door she'd sworn they'd closed last night, just in case Mason felt like wandering in while they were…

'Mason.' Her gut tied in a knot as she wrestled with her underwear. Someone seriously needed to invent bras that were easy to put on in hurry. 'What if he sees me?'

Owen came over and crouched on his haunches in front of her. He put his hand on her knee, warm and steady. His eyes were soft and kind, although she detected some panic there too. 'Calm down, sweetheart. I'm sure he won't.'

Sweetheart. Her heart squeezed at the endearment. Meanwhile, her head was full of panic and images of facing that poor little boy and trying to explain…what? That it was all only temporary. That she was leaving, just like his mum had. Her gut roiled at how that would make him feel. 'What if he does?'

'Then we'll…' Owen scraped his hand through his hair as he thought. 'Tell him you slept in the spare room.'

'Okay. Right. Great idea, Owen. The spare room that doesn't have a bed in it.' She dragged on her T-shirt and tucked it into her shorts.

But Owen just shook his head. 'We just play

it cool, okay? If we don't make a big deal out of it, he won't.'

'Are you sure?'

'Honestly? No. But what's done is done. We'll deal with it.'

He sounded certain but he looked a little shaken. She was not doing this again. She wasn't going to compromise Owen's position as a father or Mason's little heart. Or sneak around like some sort of scarlet woman. She hadn't done anything wrong, but it wasn't fair on any of them.

She hurriedly finished dressing and tiptoed across the bedroom, hopping on each foot as she slipped her sneakers on one at a time. But she overstepped and landed heavily with a thud.

'Easy does it.' Owen was quickly by her side, helping her up. 'I've never seen you like this before.'

'I've never slept in before.'

What she actually meant was, *I've never had to navigate this and I don't know what to do. Because half of me wants to wake up in this house with this man every morning. And half of me is filled with very real panic about disturbing a sleeping child...about giving everyone including myself false hope. About falling more deeply. And falling and falling...*

'I hope I didn't wake him.'

They both stood stock-still and held their

breath for a beat. Two. Owen whispered against her throat, 'See? He's fast asleep. You can make your escape.' Then he grabbed her backside and squeezed. 'Man, I love your short shorts.'

'Stop it!' she hissed, whacking away his hand as laughter bubbled from her throat, because surely she was overreacting? She gingerly pulled the door open and crept out.

But the laughter died in her throat as a tired little boy in stripy pyjamas wandered along the corridor, rubbing his eyes. He was suddenly alert the moment he recognised Carly and he ran towards her. 'Carly!'

Damn.

She shoved her hands into her pockets and tried to act as if she hadn't just had a lot of fabulous sex with his father. 'Hey, Mason.'

'Did you have a sleepover, like I did at Mia's?'

Heart rattling, she glanced over at Owen. He nodded. 'Sure she did. It's great fun, isn't it?'

She bugged her eyes at him, but then remembered they weren't making a big deal out of it. 'But now I have to go.'

'Stay for breakfast, Carly?' Mason frowned. 'Can we have pancakes, Daddy?'

'It'll take too much time, buddy. We're running a bit late today and I need to grab a shower and have a shave before work.'

The little boy's face crumpled. 'Can I show Carly my trains?'

'Another day, bud.' Owen ruffled his son's hair, but Mason slumped down on the floor in a sulk. Owen crouched down and jollied him along. 'Maybe later? Or tomorrow? Or something. We've got to a get a wriggle on this morning. How about you get dressed? Then I'll fix some toast.'

'No.' Mason folded his arms.

'Come on, mate. We've got to get a move on.' A note of frustration had slid into Owen's voice. 'It's getting late.'

Carly watched this all play out and her gut tightened. She'd seen first-hand with Mia and Harper how hard it was to be a solo parent, especially when time was limited. She also knew, from dealing with hundreds of kids herself, that getting all het up with them was unlikely to smooth things over.

Since this was all her fault, she needed to give him a hand. 'Can I do anything to help?'

Owen huffed out a breath of relief and smiled at her. 'Thanks, that would be great. Would you mind giving him a hand to get dressed while I get breakfast on?'

'Sure thing.' She offered her hand to Mason. 'Come on, champ. Let's get you ready for the day.'

The little boy's bedroom was bright and airy.

Fresh pale blue paint covered the walls. He had a red racing car bed, a set of drawers and a little desk, shelves loaded with books and two large wooden chests she imagined were filled with toys. Owen had done a fine job of creating the perfect little boy's bedroom.

She pulled open a drawer, looking for clothes. 'What are you going to wear today, Mason?'

He sauntered over and picked out a blue T-shirt and grey shorts.

After he took off his PJs she helped him into the T-shirt and then bent down and held the shorts so he could step into them.

He put his hand on her shoulder as he put one foot in and then the other. 'Are you going to sleep over tonight too?'

'No, honey. I don't think I'll be sleeping over again.' She definitely wouldn't.

'Aww. Please.'

She scanned the room to find something to distract him. Over on the desk was a drawing pad and some crayons. From a distance she could see a picture on one of the pieces of paper. She wandered over. 'Hey, what's this?'

He grinned his mischievous grin. 'I drawed you a picture.'

'Oh? That's kind. When did you do this?'

He shrugged. 'Don't know. After kindy.'

'What is it?' She could make out some rudimentary round shapes making up a number of people with circle arms and legs and tufty lines for hair.

He pointed to two small circle figures. 'My family. That's me and daddy.'

Ah. A stabbing pain lanced her chest.

'Who's that?' In the top corner, far from the little family of two, was another circle figure.

He ran his finger over it. 'Mummy. She's holding a tablet and talking to me from 'Merica.'

Poor, poor kid. Her heart stung at his words. But at least Miranda had been included in the picture, and at least Mason still spoke to her, even if he didn't get regular Mum hugs.

She looked closer at the picture and saw another figure next to the little boy wearing a crudely coloured-in blue top, very similar to that of her work uniform. She thought she might know exactly who it was, but didn't want him to say the words. She turned away, her throat suddenly tight and raw.

But he grabbed her hand and tugged her round. His stubby finger traced over the unnamed figure. 'That's you.'

She stared at the picture, trying to make sense of it and trying to work out the scramble of emotions clogging her chest. *My family.* What the hell? How could something so innocent hurt her

heart so much? She cleared her throat and nodded. *Do not cry. Do not cry.* 'That's nice.'

'Will you be my mummy too?' He looked up
at her with huge, pleading eyes.

She straightened and started to make his bed
just for something to do, so she wouldn't have
to look at him. 'You have a mummy already,
Mason.'

'My friend Tane has two mummies. I want two
mummies. I want you.'

She squeezed her eyes shut and counted slowly
to five, trying to gain some composure. She
hadn't wanted this.

Or, rather, hadn't *known* she wanted this deep
down. Hell, she'd been him once—a child with
no mother at home. She knew how desperate he
might be feeling. But, even so, she couldn't be
this little fella's mother. Hell, she didn't know
anything about parenthood. Sure, she was a good
teacher, she knew how to interest and excite kids
about being in nature. But real stuff...day-to-day
stuff? Routine and boundaries...?

And a mother? How could she be a mother
when she was exploring Vietnam? When she was
hiking the Camino in Spain?

When she opened her eyes, she saw Owen
standing in the doorway. His face was ashen, his
expression one she couldn't read.

She swallowed and turned back to Mason,

caught between the two and not knowing what to say to either of them. 'Um. You have a mummy who loves you very much. One is good. I mean, two is fine, but I can't be your mummy, Mason…' Nerves were making her babble. She had to get out of here before anything else happened. Such as breaking down in tears or her heart breaking. 'I…um… I have to go now.'

'Take it.' Mason held the picture out to her.

She glanced at Owen, then at his son. Then she took the picture in trembling hands. 'Thank you.'

She reckoned she could be in her truck in about three seconds, if she ran. Which was what she felt like doing. But she couldn't. Owen was staring at her. Mason was looking at her as if waiting for more, wanting more. Wanting what she couldn't give him.

'Bye!' Panic got the better of her and she dashed outside, where she gulped in fresh air, hoping it would calm her down.

It didn't. She was rattled. Panicked. What confusion had she caused in that poor little boy by her selfish behaviour? She'd wanted to make love with Owen. She'd wanted to bask in his attention, to fill her need. But at what cost to Mason? To her own heart?

She ran to her truck and dragged the door open. As she was climbing in, she heard Owen's voice behind her. 'God, Carly. I'm so sorry. I didn't know he was going to draw that.'

She looked up and saw his hair all ruffled from their lovemaking—and no doubt from a good deal of scrubbing his hand through it, trying to explain things to Mason.

She put her hand to her chest, more to calm her racing heart than anything. 'What did we expect, though? All this time spent together, camping, kayaking. Being friends. Being close. He must have seen you being…happy.' Because, yes, they'd both fed a need. Last night was the closest she'd been to happy in a long time.

She put her head on the steering wheel. 'I'm sorry. I'm so sorry.'

CHAPTER TWELVE

OWEN WATCHED THE flash of emotions rushing behind Carly's eyes just before she dropped her head onto the steering wheel, and his heart just about stalled in his chest. She was hurting and Mason was confused.

Hell, he was confused.

It had all gone too far. They'd been grasping something for themselves, but the ramifications rippled out like a stone thrown into the ocean, causing who knew what damage to each of them? A friendship. Sex. More. Reaching. Hoping. And now Mason was starting to hope for the impossible too.

At all costs, he had to protect his little boy.

Yet he looked at Carly, hurting too, and his heart pumped again, hard and fast. She was… everything. This woman was the closest thing to perfect he'd ever met. His head buzzed. His chest felt as if the world were pressing in on it.

He probably should let her drive away, but he couldn't leave it like this.

'Carly.' He gripped the open window frame. 'Look at me.'

'You're late for work.' She groaned into the steering wheel. 'And I have to go.'

'Not yet. We need to talk.'

'Yeah.' She raised her head and looked at him, eyes bruised with worry. 'So, what do we do now?'

'I don't know.' He was paralysed by anguish, because what he wanted and what they had to do were completely at odds. There was no way out of this.

'What do you want from me, Owen? What do you want?'

What the hell? Wasn't that obvious now? He wanted to wake up with her every day. He wanted a woman who wanted to be in his life.

But he couldn't put that kind of pressure on her. 'I want you to be happy.'

Her eyes blazed as she shook her head. 'Wrong answer. What do *you* want? From me? From us?'

'What does it matter what I *want*?' What was the use in explaining it all? Each time he thought he knew where he stood, the rug was pulled from under him. Women didn't stay. 'Will what I want make a difference? You're going, Carly, and I totally respect that, but we have to be honest about it. We're kidding ourselves that we can share our lives in the short term without getting hurt. I care about you. Too much.' He couldn't watch someone walk away again and allow his heart to be shattered for the third time. Hell, he'd only just recovered from the emotional whiplash Miranda had caused. 'There isn't any "us". There can't be.'

She pressed her lips together. Her bottom lip trembled. 'What was last night, then? The "I want you"… The running down the jetty desperate for me… All of this…' She waved her hand between them.

Good question. He shook his head as he tried to control his breathing and his thoughts and failed on both accounts. 'It's reckless. It's…dangerous. To me and to my boy. It's false hope.'

'What do you mean?'

'Hell, Carly. Isn't it obvious? I want to ask you to stay. To give up your dreams and be here with me and Mason. But that's not fair on you. You have a dream and a plan, and you have to be true to yourself.'

Her eyebrows rose. 'You want me to stay?'

'No. I want to be…' He'd come to the truth of it now. Pain lanced his chest. '*Enough* that you'd stay.' His gaze connected with hers and he saw the torment running through her mind. She hadn't planned to get involved. She hadn't planned any of this. They should have been more careful. 'I know you have to leave.'

She kept on looking at him. Silence stretched.

Then her eyes lit up briefly, as if she'd found the answer. 'You could…wait for me?'

'How long do I wait? How long do Mason and I put our lives on hold?' He knew how long. He knew what it was like to hope and then have those hopes smashed. He wasn't going to give up his agency this time, hand over the dregs of his power to someone else. 'Even you don't know how long you're going to be away. You have no plans to come back permanently, you said so yourself. So, no, I really couldn't wait. I've played that game before, Carly. I'm tired of waiting, of putting my own plans on hold.'

Her eyes fluttered closed and she inhaled, her chest stuttering, then exhaled slowly. 'I understand.'

'I don't think you do. Hell, I know you've been through so much pain, and I know how much you want to grab some happiness. I know how much you deserve all of it too. Everything. You deserve a life that is created by you, to be cherished and loved, and you deserve a cheerleader to support you through it all. Someone who's free, who could maybe come along with you and watch you blossom.

'Hell, I'd love to be that person. I really would. But I can't. You know that. Mason's had too much upheaval, and now we're just getting settled.' He couldn't throw it all away, uproot the foundations he'd so carefully laid…not for someone who might not stay around. Because they never did in the end.

'Oh, Owen.' She blinked, her eyes swimming in tears. 'I could…maybe I could stay.'

'What? No.' He knew what it must have taken for her to say that. To reach out and try, to offer to put her hopes on hold for him. He closed his eyes as possibility swam in front of him, and he wanted so much to grab hold of it. But how could he do that again? How could he put Mason at such a risk?

'When I was a kid, I watched my mother leave and there was nothing I could do to stop her. My whole life was blown apart, my safety net in tatters. I didn't understand that it was something she needed to do, I just thought I'd done something wrong. That I wasn't good enough and that was why she was leaving me. And then I had to watch it happen to my kid. Have you any idea how that feels? To watch someone break your child's heart and be able to do nothing? I couldn't make her stay…couldn't make either of them stay. I can't let him go through that again. Hell… I can't do it to myself.'

'I'm not Miranda.' She was shaking now, and he hated that he made her be like this. But he had to break this off. It was the right thing to do, even if it hurt like hell now.

'I know you're not, and I know you have every good intention, Carly. She did too, she's not a monster. But I can't take that risk and ask you to give up your dreams and stay just a little longer. Hope you'll settle with me, with us. Hope you'll forget your plans, and that you'll change and fit into our life. All it does is put off the inevitable. I'll just end up waiting for the end.'

She slid her hand over his. 'There doesn't have to be an end.'

'Really? Not when you start to get itchy feet again? When you realise this small family life isn't the kind of wild adventure you'd been planning?'

'No.' She shook her head quickly. 'It doesn't have to end like that.'

'But it will. I won't tell myself lies and I certainly won't tell them to my son. It's best if we finish it all now. That way you're free to leave and we can…' *Recover.*

He'd seen the *Under Offer* banner slapped across the Camp Rāwhiti sign. If the camp, all her island history and Mia and Harper weren't enough to keep her here, how could he be?

Or…maybe he was tarnishing her with the same brush as his ex-wife and his mother. Maybe he was being unfair. Perhaps she would stick to her word. Perhaps she would come back to them. Maybe they could reach some sort of deal.

But she pressed her lips together, as if holding in something she didn't want to escape in front of him. Then she managed, 'Are you saying you don't want to try to reach a compromise? That you don't care about me? Because I care about you, Owen.'

'Of course, I care about you, Carly. You're amazing. Beautiful. Funny. Sexy. Bright. So damned bright. I lo—' He slammed his mouth shut as he realised what he was about to say.

Love.

Now, that was a wild notion. But, hell, the only thing that could cause this amount of hurt, confusion and chaos stemmed from love. He'd tried to protect himself, had tried to put up walls, but she'd broken them down with her smile, her touch and her kisses.

He loved her.

And it was the worst possible thing he could ever do. It made him desperate, it blurred his logic. It derailed him. Look at him now, trying to make a deal with himself. Trying to think of ways he could have it all when, deep down, he knew he just couldn't.

Because he'd loved before and he'd been left behind, trying to mop up the mess. 'I have to care for myself and my son.'

'You're hiding behind Mason. Making excuses not to jump in.' She shook her head and snatched her hand back, her eyes wild. 'You say you care about me, but you don't want to wait or make promises. And now you're saying you won't let me stay either. You're pushing me away. What the hell kind of care is that?'

'I'm not going to make promises that will clip your wings, Carly. Promises that will turn into regret, or a bind you want to shrug off. We really don't know each other.' If he told himself that enough, he might start to believe it. He knew her enough to lose his heart to her. Knew her enough that he wanted the best for her. He loved her.

Hell.

'I know what I feel.' She put her hand to her heart, and he suddenly wanted to hear what more she had to say about that.

'Which is what?'

'I like you. A lot. I really do care about you and about Mason. We could at least try. We could do video calling.' But even as she said it her hopeful expression dissolved and her shoulders slumped, telling him she realised what she was suggesting. 'Like Miranda.'

'Daddy! Daddy! Mummy's calling.' As if on cue, and with the worst possible timing in the world, Mason ran out of the house waving his digital tablet, his eyes dancing with excitement as the screen lit up with light and sound.

Mason. He shouldn't be watching this. And Miranda most definitely shouldn't be.

Owen closed his eyes and tried to control the rush of panic, of pain and, yes, of love. The joy of seeing his son so animated mingled with the loss of Carly.

Once again, his gaze connected with hers and he saw, with that one plaintive statement from Mason, that she knew he was right. He wasn't about to make a deal that could hurt him or his boy. He would always put Mason before his own needs, wants or desires. Always.

He dragged his eyes away, but not before committing her beautiful face to memory. The eyes that bore into him as if she was reaching into his soul and making him question everything he believed to be true. The mouth that made him laugh with her jokes and that broke him open with her kisses. The wild red-gold hair.

Love. It sure as hell made you crazy.

Then he turned to Mason and dragged up a smile and jolly tone he wasn't sure he could maintain for long. 'Hey, bud. Just chatting.' The screen had gone dark. 'Sorry, she's hung up. Give me the tablet and we can dial in. But we'll have to be quick or we'll be very late for kindy.'

That was what was important. He needed to keep the lines of communication open between

Mason and his mother and a solid routine. Nothing else.

He took a step towards his son, who raised his chubby fist and waved happily at Carly, showing her his tablet. 'It's Mummy!'

But Owen didn't wave, he didn't look back to see Carly's reaction, not when he heard her sharp intake of breath, the soft sob in her throat, the roar of the truck's engine and the tyres on gravel.

He didn't look even when he was desperate for one last glance. Because he was an idiot, not a masochist.

Walking those few steps was one of the hardest things he'd ever done, because she'd wanted him to make a promise and it would have been so easy to agree. To put off the pain for another day just to save himself from it today.

Sure, we'll wait a few weeks. Months. A year. We'll sit on the sidelines until you're ready to come back to us, a different person with different ideas and expectations.

He wasn't going to do that to Mason.

And he certainly wasn't going to do it to himself.

Carly fisted away the tears that blurred her vision. It wasn't such a great idea to drive when she was crying this hard, but she'd had no choice. She'd had to leave.

Bloody man.

Bloody beautiful, amazing man. Who loved so hard, he'd protect his son from anything.

Protect himself too, because he'd been hurt in the past. His mother had left, his wife had gone and he couldn't take that risk again.

Love.

Had she imagined it? Had it been on the tip of his tongue? Her heart had squeezed in hope, and then crumpled, because who loves you and then pushes you away?

Don't go.

She'd watched each step he'd taken away from her and had willed him to turn round. Just once. Just one time, so she could look at his face. But he hadn't. She'd watched his rigid back and taut shoulders retreat from her, had watched him bend to pick up Mason and hold him close, and every part of her had craved his hug, had wanted those arms around her waist, those lips on her cheek. She'd wanted to run to him, hammer her fists on his back and make him promise to wait for her. Hell, she wasn't going for ever.

But she was going long enough that he'd forget her.

It looked almost as if Mason had forgotten his second mummy request already. She hadn't missed the excitement in his eyes at the thought of his mother. Who knew, if she stayed, Mason's and Miranda's contact might fade…and she knew first-hand how important it was to keep those ties sacrosanct.

But now? Her heart had been blown into tiny pieces all over again. Her chest hurt. Her throat hurt. She'd tried to keep her heart out of it, had tried to convince herself she could leave unscathed and untouched by them. She didn't want to care for them this much. Didn't want to imagine the next few weeks without them. But Owen had made it clear that, whatever she said, he was going to reject her.

She pulled up behind her cottage and saw Mia waiting for her, her hair whipping around in the breeze. Summer was turning to autumn and, as usual around the equinox, with big sea swells and squally storms. Everything was unsettled. Tumultuous. The way she felt right now.

No, please. Not now. Not this.

Carly's heart sank at the sight of Mia because she knew she'd be forced to talk to her when she just wanted to hide away and cry. But time was running out, so she swallowed down her pain, wiped her eyes and found her sister-in-law a smile as she jumped down from the truck. 'Hey.'

Mia frowned. 'What's the matter, hun?'

It was plain she couldn't keep anything from her. 'It's nothing. I'm fine. Why are you here? Is everything okay?'

'Look at you, always worrying over everything.' Mia grinned and cupped Carly's cheek, peering closer at her face. 'Are you sure you're okay? You don't look fine to me.'

Please don't ask. I'll cry all over again.

'Oh, you know.' Carly sniffed and wiped her nose on her sleeve because she'd just used up the box of tissues she kept in her glove compartment.

'Oh, honey, I do. I do. Grief hits us in weird ways. I still get overwhelmed by it sometimes.' Clearly Mia thought Carly's tears were for Raff and his parents. 'Um...we arranged for me to come collect some of your things this morning.'

'Oh. Yes. I forgot.' But it was Owen, not Raff, who had made her forget her grief, her history and even her plans. Or, rather, she'd been desperate enough to put them on hold for him. She'd almost bargained herself out of her trip. Tried to make rash promises she knew neither of them could or should keep. Tried to get one more family to accept her and love her. And for one mad moment she'd been prepared to give everything up for them.

It really did look as though she was destined to be on her own. Alone.

But she'd been there before and she could do it again. If only her heart would ever stop hurting.

Mia was still chattering. 'Countdown to the big day's started, so it's only natural you'll feel a bit wobbly. Don't forget, this is your big adventure. You've been planning it for so long, dreaming about it ever since you cut it short to come here with Raff.'

'Everything's in here.' Carly opened the door to her cosy lounge and gestured to the piles of things she'd been supposed to pack last night. But, instead, she'd spent that time with Owen.

Together they put her treasures into boxes and secured the lids with sticky tape. They were just filling the last one when Mia picked up the kauri jewellery box. 'Oh. Isn't this the box Raff made for your wedding present?'

'Yes.' Carly inhaled deeply and steadied her ragged breaths. 'I want you to keep it for me.'

Mia opened the lid and gasped. 'Oh. Your wedding ring.'

'Yes.' Was this the right thing to do? Yes, it was. She had to put a line under everything. Raff, this house, Owen. She had to take her place in the world. Carly Edwards…whoever she was… was waiting to blossom. 'I don't… Please don't take this the wrong way. I will never forget your brother. But I have to step out into the world as me. Not as a widow.'

'I understand. I really do. I get it.' Mia wrapped her into a tight hug. 'Please promise me you'll have lots of fun. I want you to message me daily with updates. We can video call. You can show me and Harper all the amazing places you visit.'

Video call…like Mason and his mum. Like countless others who found a way to connect with people they loved and cared for despite the miles keeping them apart. Like she'd offered Owen.

She sighed. 'I will. Will you be okay without me?'

Mia grinned. 'We're two amazing, strong women. We've got this.'

'Yes, we have.' Carly found Mia a smile. She was right; they'd both faced impossible sadness and survived it. They had a future to look forward to. Happiness waited for them.

But whatever else happened, and despite herself, Carly knew she would carry her losses with her wherever she went. The memories of Raff and his family, and now of Owen too.

Because the man she'd thought might heal her heart had broken it instead.

CHAPTER THIRTEEN

Owen stood at the harbour and watched the ferry depart, taking with it Mia and Carly, and any hope that things could be fixed between them.

She hadn't seen him there. Hadn't come out on deck. Hadn't said goodbye—not a single word. Hadn't even come in with Mia to drop Harper off at the surgery.

They'd managed to avoid each other over the last few days. He'd even stayed away from her leaving party, telling everyone that Mason was under the weather. Truth was, he hadn't been able to say goodbye. He'd done that too many times in his life already and this time, he knew, would be the worst.

And yet here he was today, unable to let her go. But he had to.

The wind picked up, sending an old brown paper bag scuttling across the ground. The clouds threatened rain. He put his hands on Mason's and Harper's shoulders and caught their attention away from feeding the baby ducks that hung around on the water. 'Come on, kids. Let's get back inside. There's a storm on its way.'

'From what I hear, it's a big one too.' Anahera slipped her arm into his and walked with them back to the surgery. But his focus was on the boat. 'I hope the ferry's going to be okay.'

Anahera squeezed his arm and smiled softly. 'You mean, you hope Carly's going to be okay.'

Busted. 'Yes. Mia too. Obviously.'

'Of course, Mia. But Carly mainly.' She raised her eyebrows, letting him know she'd guessed and understood. She shivered as a cold wind whipped round their heads, dragging strands of grey hair from her clip. 'It's an easterly storm, unusual for here, but they always bring a good dousing and even cyclones. We need to batten down the hatches. And my hair.'

'Cyclones and ferries aren't a good mix.' Owen craned his head to catch a final glimpse of the boat disappearing into rough-looking seas.

'It'll hit us first. Hopefully they'll be on the mainland by the time it reaches the city.' Anahera pushed open the surgery door and they all clambered in. The pressure of the wind made him lean hard against the door to close it. Anahera bent and opened the children's play box in the reception waiting room. 'How do you feel about being the island's first responder now?'

'Good. I think. Everyone knows what they're

doing, right? It's just following protocols. We'll be fine.' His heart fluttered with pride at having been asked, but also with a little trepidation. People were depending on him. 'If the storm gets worse, or there's likely to be a threat to life from flooding, we evacuate to the camp.'

His receptionist nodded. 'For the next three months. After the new owner moves in, we'll have to rethink that emergency plan.'

'I've called a meeting for next week to discuss it all.'

She looked up from pulling out some building blocks for Harper. 'You'll make a great leader here, Owen. You've got good ideas and great intentions. I'd say you've made it your home.'

'I hope so. I love it here.'

She pierced him with one of those stares only wise women could get away with. 'But you'll miss having Carly here to help.'

I miss her, full stop. I love her.

He couldn't deny that any longer. Although, he'd yet to say it fully out loud. But now he'd watched her leave and there was no chance for them.

'You're soft on her.' It was a statement, not a question. His receptionist was astute.

Or... had he actually said it out loud? 'She's a great woman, Anahera.'

She gave a nod in agreement. 'She'll be back.'

In two years or something.

'I hope she has an amazing time.'

'You hope she changes her mind.' Anahera winked then patted his shoulder. 'What will be, will be, Doc. These things have a habit of sorting themselves out.'

Yes, but not always in my favour. In fact, never.

He was about to reply when a loud howling noise ripped through the air, making Harper jump in surprise. Her little face crumpled and she started to sob.

Owen pushed his thoughts about Carly back and focused on the little girl. 'Hey. It's just the wind. It's okay. It's okay.'

He sat down and pulled her onto his lap, cradling her and rocking her the way he'd always done with Mason. Meanwhile, his big boy son played happily with some trains. Anahera stood up and busied herself at the reception desk.

There was a strange feeling in the atmosphere. Owen felt as if he was in some weird kind of limbo. He felt unsettled, unsure, as if he was holding his breath, waiting...

Maybe it was the static from the encroaching storm. Maybe it was his heart, not quite believing that she'd gone.

The phone rang.

Carly? His chest hurt.

Anahera answered.

Owen looked up expectantly. But why was he hoping? He'd just watched her sail away.

Anahera shook her head, as if reading his mind. 'That's your last patient cancelling their appointment. No one wants to come out today and I don't blame them. I've just seen on the on-line news that there's a cyclone likely.'

Not surprising, given that the walls felt as though they were trembling, the windows rattling in their frames. 'You should go home.'

'This building's safer than my house in a storm. I'll go put the kettle on.' The lights flickered, then went out. Anahera sighed. 'Power cut. Great. We need a generator here, Doc.'

'Add it to the list.' Still holding Harper, Owen shuffled to standing and dashed to the window. The yachts in the marina were being tossed about like toy boats in a kid's bath. Every building was dark. The flag on the flagpole whirled in a brutal, jagged dance. More debris tumbled down the street.

All he could see, far out on the water, were huge waves—white-topped and violent—and a sky as black as night. It was three-thirty. It shouldn't be this dark.

What if something happened to them in the storm? What if...? No. He wasn't going there. He turned to Anahera, 'We'd know if there was a problem with the ferry, right? We'd hear about it.'

Anahera stretched her arms out to take Harper from him and cooed as she rocked the girl back to sleep. 'We'd be first to find out. They'd radio in.'

It couldn't happen twice, not to the same family—two boating disasters. No, they'd be fine. The women would be drinking cocktails in an hour, celebrating signing the papers that set them free.

While here he was, hostage to his heart.

'Daddy, can I have a snack?'

Thank God for kids. They kept you sane and gave you a reason to focus. He wandered through to the lunchroom and grabbed some fruit, cut it into pieces and gave it to them. Then he played trains for what felt like an interminable amount of time.

The clock ticked. The wind howled. The frames rattled. Then the rain started, thick, greasy drops on the corrugated iron roof. It felt as if someone was hammering into his skull.

What if something happened to her?

He wouldn't be able to endure what she'd been through when she'd lost her husband. She was stronger than he was. She'd loved Raff and lost him. Had prayed he'd come back to her. Had waited. And waited.

Was this a little of how she'd felt? No. He couldn't imagine the horrors she'd been through. And yet…he couldn't think straight or be rational. He wanted to rip open the door, dive into the turbulent water and go find her.

He wanted to hold her and kiss her.

What if something happened to her?

He'd go out of his mind. All their missed chances—all that love, days of laughter, sexy sleepless nights. Her warmth, her skin. Her optimism. Her strength. He'd let her go. No, he'd made her go.

He couldn't live like this. He couldn't…

These things have a habit of sorting themselves out.

How, when she was following her own path and it certainly wasn't converging with his any time soon?

But maybe he could forge a way.

How? He didn't have any answers.

But he knew he wanted to try.

He'd pushed her away without giving her the time and space to talk things through. He'd knee-jerk reacted to panic that his son was getting too close to her. All that protectiveness had made him wary.

He'd been an idiot. Why hadn't he listened? Why hadn't he talked?

Because he'd been too scared to take a risk.

Like the risk she was taking by leaving this island. Like the risk he'd taken coming here. Like the risk he was taking, agreeing to be the island's first responder. Hell, he was happy to carry the weight of everyone here on his shoulders, but too cowardly to allow one person into his heart, into his life…

How was that even living, being scared, being closed off? He'd already taken a lot of risks. What was one more if it brought her back to him?

His chest flickered with hope. Maybe if he just talked to her, one last time. Maybe if he said yes to the video calls. Maybe if he was just brave enough to take a step.

He turned his back to the window. 'Anahera, do you think you'd be able to look after the kids tomorrow?'

'Sure, thing. Why?'

'I need to make a trip into the city.'

I need to get her back. Somehow.

'Of course—' She was interrupted by both their bleepers sounding shrilly at the same time.

Ferry run aground North Bay.

He looked up and saw Anahera's ashen face. And his heart stopped.

'Sign here and here.' The officious lawyer pointed a perfectly polished nail at the yellow stickies on the forms, indicating where they had to sign away the camp.

'Here we go.' Mia grinned as she scribbled her name. 'This is a good thing, Carly.'

'I know. I just…have a funny feeling.' Carly looked out of the window on the top floor of the tower block, over the city buildings and out to the Hauraki Gulf. She'd hoped it would be glittering today, but it was rough and foreboding. Thank goodness she didn't get seasick, because their crossing had been dire.

Mia followed her gaze. 'About what?'

'I don't know. Everything.' She shivered. 'And I'm not used to air conditioning. I'm freezing.'

'It's actually really warm in here.' Mia stroked Carly's back. 'It's probably just nerves. Try and look at it as excitement. We're going to go and drink cocktails, get drunk and silly and dance and then tomorrow night you're off on an adventure.'

She didn't feel adventurous. She felt…weird. Lost. Alone. Her head and heart kept slanting back to Owen and Mason.

'Sure, must be that.' Carly signed her name in the numerous places the lawyer indicated then shook her hand.

'Congratulations, ladies. The sale is now unconditional. Contracts are signed. If all goes to plan—and I don't see why it won't—you'll settle in a month.'

Mia squealed. 'So that's it? It's sold?'

'It is.' The lawyer nodded and grinned.

Mia's eyes grew huge. 'I'm so going kitchen shopping. Right now. Come with me! Help me choose something very swanky for my little cottage.'

So, they did. And, even though it felt endlessly domestic, Carly enjoyed it. More, she enjoyed seeing her sister-in-law happy and excited for the first time in too long.

'Let's celebrate.' As the sun started to set over Auckland, Mia hooked her arm into Carly's and pulled her into a bar that overlooked the waterfront. Out on the horizon the darkening clouds dumped fat fingers of rain into the unsettled ocean. Carly's stomach felt as choppy as the sea.

Was this all such a good idea?

When their champagne arrived, Mia picked up her glass and held it to Carly's. 'I never thought I'd be in this situation, doing this. Saying goodbye to the house I grew up in, to the camp that grounded me, that taught me to love and respect nature…even though she can be an evil mistress sometimes.' Her eyes darted towards the tumbling waves and they both knew she was talking about the accident that had ripped their family away. 'But I'm glad I have you by my side, Carly. Even when you're overseas, I know you'll be there for me. I'm glad I have you.'

Carly's throat felt ragged and sore. 'I'm glad I

have you too. Thank you for being there for me through everything.'

'You were a gift my brother brought home, and I couldn't thank him for a better present than you. You were there for me in the worst time of my life and the best. You're the best godparent for Harper. And a total all-round wonder woman.'

'Aww, shucks.' Carly clinked her glass, hoping she looked better than she felt. Maybe she did get seasick after all. Maybe it just took a little while to settle. 'To us. The Edwards girls.'

'Sisters by family, friends by choice.' Mia took a sip of her champagne and laughed. 'I could get used to this. It's a good feeling when you know you can splash out every now and then on something frivolous like bubbles.'

'Wait…isn't champagne an essential food group?' Carly couldn't help but laugh too. 'Sorry, I know I need to start focusing on the positives. I've got financial stability. I've got independence. I'm very resilient…hell, I could face just about anything now. Not that I want to.' But her heart ached for what she'd left behind. 'I want to be happy. I want to be part of something.'

'You have your whole life in front of you. I envy you a bit.' Mia sighed and twiddled with her flute stem. 'All that opportunity. Doing new things, meeting new people.'

'Oh? This isn't like you. I thought you loved Rāwhiti, and you adore Harper.'

'Oh yes, of course, and I wouldn't change that at all. But there's something missing.'

Carly frowned. How had she missed the fact that her sister-in-law was feeling like this? Because she'd been too absorbed in her own woes. 'You're a woman of means now. You can travel, do things. What do you want, Mia, right now?'

Her friend looked straight at Carly and sighed. 'Oh, man. I want good sex. And a lot of it.'

Carly spluttered her champagne and had to wipe her mouth with a napkin. 'Wow. I wasn't expecting that. You never talk about it. Never talk about Mia's dad or that night.'

'Which was the last time I had sex. Not that I'm counting.' Mia bugged her eyes. 'There's simply no point in talking about him. I tried to find him and I couldn't. He's gone. I've accepted that.'

'There are other men.'

'On Rāwhiti? I doubt it. You've snagged the only decent single guy there. Or, rather, had snagged.'

Another choke on the bubbles and Carly snorted. 'No snagging happened.'

'Just good sex, then? I'm so jealous.' Mia giggled. 'Lucky duck. You never know, you might meet the next man of your dreams in Greece. Or Spain. Or…'

Carly's thoughts immediately jumped to Owen. Again. No matter how hard she tried, she couldn't forget him. She'd always measured every man against Raff, and none had ever compared. But he was gone. Owen was now the yardstick by which she'd compare every subsequent lover.

And she'd left him behind. A sharp pain lanced her chest. She missed him so much.

'Talking of my daughter's father, I really should check in.' Mia pulled out her phone and scanned the screen. 'No messages. I'll give Owen a call, just to make sure they're okay.'

'Give him my love.' Carly closed her mouth quickly.

Mia blinked and then peered at her, her eyes searching, guessing and then realising. She gave Carly a soft, sad kind of smile, then she started to scroll and pressed call.

Carly imagined him sitting round the fire about now, toasting marshmallows for Harper and Mason. Reading them books before bed. She thought about him pottering around the kitchen, kayaking, painting, tending to the injured with soot streaked across his face. She thought about the rhythmic rise and fall of his chest after very good sex. She wouldn't tell Mia about that.

She imagined his neat spruced-up cottage. His special scent. The touch of his fingertips. His laugh. The care for Mason. The intention only ever to put his son first.

She thought about the way he'd looked at her as he'd slid inside her as if she was everything. Thought about the gentle touch of his fingers in her hair.

Did his heart hurt like hers did?

She'd wanted to reach for him, but he'd closed himself off. She wanted… Oh, she didn't know what she wanted. She was so confused. And, anyway, it didn't matter what she wanted. He'd made up his mind. He'd set her free.

Stupid thing was, she didn't want to be.

Give him my love.

It hit her then, deep in her heart, that she did love him. Loved them both. But he was pushing her away and she was wilfully going. How could she walk away from love, the one thing she'd craved her whole life?

How long would it take for her to forget his smile?

Never.

How long would it take for her heart to heal?

Mia put her phone down and frowned. 'That's strange. He's not answering.'

'He's probably busy. You know what it's like with two small kids. He won't have his phone with him all the time.'

'Yes. Probably right.' Mia slid her phone back

into her bag and glanced up at the TV screen in the corner.

Her eyebrows rose. 'Oh. You see that? The storm over Rāwhiti has knocked out the power. That's why he's not answering. Apparently, there's a cyclone on the way.'

Heart hammering, Carly whipped round to look. 'I hope they're okay. I hope they're coping without us.'

'You wrote the emergency plan. You know how good it is. If they follow the rule book, they'll be fine.'

'Yes. Yes, you're right. I can't spend my whole life looking back and panicking at the slightest thing. But what if...?' Carly knew her grip on Mia's arm was tight but she couldn't stop herself. What if he wasn't okay, as Raff hadn't been? How could she lose him too?

She felt as if she was going to be sick as pain roiled through her, piercing her heart. But he didn't want her. He'd sent her on her adventure. He hadn't looked back at her.

The cosy fireside image died, and she imagined him now battling the storm with the kids, securing the windows and doors... Was Wallace-Wilma okay too? Maybe he was taking them all to the camp, just as the rule book said. Hunkering down in safety with her friends, her family.

Then she imagined him taking so much care

with any injured people. Keeping them safe. Walking forward into risk, danger and adventure. She thought of the islanders relying on him, the way they'd relied on her. She thought of all that going on without her. All that love, care and community. Her home.

And Owen. The kingpin of it all. A beacon of hope.

A sexy beacon of hope. She smiled, even though she was concerned for him and for the islanders in this weather bomb.

She envied him, admired him and loved him.

She loved him.

Oh, God. She loved him. The man who thought his life was too small for her when what he was doing was the most amazing thing of all…building a life, a real, happy life, that nurtured his son and helped him thrive. What could be better than that?

And suddenly her own adventure felt small and unnecessary. She didn't have to fly halfway around the world to find out who she was. She knew who she was. She was Carly Edwards, first responder of Rāwhiti Island. Carly Edwards, lover of Owen Cooper. Carly Edwards, a woman capable of many, many things, including loving this man and receiving that love back tenfold. She didn't just want to look back…she wanted to go back.

'I think I've made a mistake,' she whispered to Mia's back. 'I think I love him.'

But her friend was standing completely still, staring at a red banner running across the bottom of the screen.

Breaking news... Ferry runs aground at Rāwhiti Island. Storm hampers rescue efforts.

Carly's heart jolted.

Then she grabbed her bag and shook her friend gently. 'We have to go back, Mia. Now. We have to get back to Rāwhiti.'

She had to get back to the man she loved and wanted to spend the rest of her life with.

If it wasn't too late.

CHAPTER FOURTEEN

CARLY STOOD NEXT to Mia at the edge of the helipad on top of the ambulance control building. Rain lashed their faces as wind whipped around them, biting their skin. She wrapped her raincoat more tightly around her, but it didn't make any difference. Rain found a way of getting in, made worse by the chopper's rotors turning each drop into a barb pricking her skin.

Mia shivered next to her and swiped her hand across her eyes. 'We're never going to get there in this weather.'

'We just have to pray for a decent weather window. That's all we need. Thirty minutes to get there. But we have to be ready to go.' Carly shifted her weight, her rucksack straps digging into her back.

'Thank goodness you're well enough connected to grab us a lift with these guys.'

'As soon as I heard they were trying to rescue some of the ferry passengers, I knew they'd dispatch a chopper.'

'Right.' Mia nodded towards two paramedics stomping across the tarmac. 'Here goes nothing.'

Bent almost double against the downdraft and the wind, they followed the two men and huddled next to each other until it was their turn to climb in.

Carly went first, hauling herself up into the helicopter's main body. The two paramedics were already seated, not talking. The only sound was the roar of the engine. And was it her imagination, or was the helicopter actually rocking in the wild wind?

Stomping on her nerves, she found two empty seats across from them, buckled in, put on her headphones and listened to the pilot talking them through the plan. 'There's been some casualties over there. Sounds bad. As soon as I get a chance to go, we'll go. Be ready. It's going to be a bumpy ride.'

Mia climbed in and sat down next to Carly, her face ashen. She made a weird sort of sound.

Carly glanced at her. Was she scared of what they were going to find on their beloved island?

Of course she was. Carly was too. Scared of what she might find and what she might have already lost.

She slid her hand over Mia's and squeezed, summoning up an optimism she hadn't known she had. 'Hey, it's going to be okay.'

But her friend's eyes were fixed on one of the paramedics in the seat opposite—a tall guy with cropped hair. Good-looking. 'I don't think so.'

The weird thing was, he looked spooked too. Then he blinked and turned away, one hand pressing on the headphones as the pilot began to speak again.

Their panic was infectious. Carly's heart rate ramped up, her palms starting to sweat. Now it wasn't just a case of, would Owen have her back? It was more a question of, were they going to get there alive?

Owen stood in the pitching fishing boat, shivering in the cold and rain as he helped lift his patient onto the Rāwhiti Camp jetty, being careful not to jolt her in any way. The wood was slippery and slick with water. The noise from the wind was almost deafening but its ferocity had definitely lessened over the last few minutes. The rain blurred his vision but it didn't stop him seeing the flotilla of boats bringing back the wounded from the ferry. The storm might be dying down, but his work was far from over.

'Careful!' he shouted, so the wind didn't steal his words, and the greeting party of island helpers heard his instructions. 'I've given her some pain relief and stabilised the fractures. Get her up to the camp and keep her warm until I get back. She's going to need an evacuation.'

One of the helpers shouted back, 'The chopper's just landed, Doc. Paramedics are on their way down.'

'Thank God. The ferry's listing badly and there's more injured to come.' But the sense of relief of not being alone almost made his legs give way. It was one thing to be a first responder, but another to be the only medic on the island. He couldn't go back out on the boat to help rescue the victims and stay here to tend to the injured all at the same time.

He needed more experienced helpers. He needed Mia.

No, he needed Carly. For her strength and clear head. For her kisses. For her warm open-heartedness.

God, he missed her.

'Okay, Doc. We've got her. You're free to go.'

Free? He was tied to Carly for ever. His heart was hers. And, as soon as this nightmare was over, he was going to find her and tell her. Promise that he'd wait for her, no matter how long, or that he'd give everything up, and Mason and him would go with her. Anything to be with her. Whatever she wanted. Because a love like this didn't come round twice in a lifetime.

He turned back to the boat, wishing he didn't

have to go back out there to the swollen, dark sea and the screams for help. But he pushed against the jetty and let the boat glide deeper into the sea.

'Owen! Owen!'

He looked up and blinked and for a moment his heart almost exploded. The rain was definitely blurring his vision, or exhaustion was making him see mirages of hope, if he thought Carly was running towards him in a bright yellow raincoat, her hair flying behind her, like some kind of superhero.

No. It was not Carly, just wishful thinking. He blinked again and watched the chasm of water between the jetty and the boat grow.

'Owen! Wait!'

It was her voice. His body went into some kind of shut-down. At least that must have been why he couldn't move, not one muscle.

It was Carly, and she was haring down the jetty. In one smooth motion, she jumped into the boat. He couldn't read her expression. 'Owen.'

'Carly.' His heart was the first thing that came back to life. Hope was a flower opening in his chest. 'What the hell?'

She gripped the side of the rocking boat. 'Where are the kids? Harper and Mason. Where's your boy?'

Her first thought was for his son. 'At the camp with Anahera.'

She put her hand onto her heart and nodded, sighing. 'Good. Right. What do you need?'

You.

He wasn't sure what she meant. Why was she here and not in the city? Why had she come back? 'Um. We've got to get back to the ferry before it sinks. There might be some people who need immediate life support.'

Like me.

She grabbed the steering wheel. 'Okay. Let's go. Tell me where to head.'

She'd come to help. Of course she had. She'd come back to the island when it needed her. She hadn't come back for him.

After a stomach-churning trip, he pointed to the ferry as it started to lurch sideways. 'Don't get any closer. Stay here.'

'What about the passengers? We've got to get them. Save them.' Her hand was over her mouth as they watched the boat's white hull slip deeper under the water. She edged the boat closer, but he made her stop. 'No, Carly. No closer.'

'We've got to help them, Owen. Please. Please.'

'No.' The white paint was subsumed now. 'It's not safe for us to be there. If we get any closer, we could be dragged under too. This time, you don't put your life on the line. I'm not going to lose you.'

'No. No...' Her body crumpled and she swayed

with their pitching boat. Ugly waves thrashed the sides, spilling over and soaking their feet.

He held her arms and held her steady until she broke and sobbed against him. 'It's not fair. It's not fair.'

And his heart broke along with hers. He wrapped his arms around her and stroked her hair. He thought about the way her husband had died, the emotions all wrapped up in that and how witnessing this would be unbearable. 'I know, darling, it isn't fair. It just isn't. But we've done what we can.'

'It's not enough.' But she gripped his shoulders, trembling, tears streaming down her face. And he let her cry and cry until all that was left were dry sobs.

A smaller boat with a bright white light slowly made its way towards them. The coastguard. Owen reluctantly let go of Carly, leaned over the side and shouted to the people on board, 'What's the score? How many people are left on there?'

'All evacuated. Captain here says he was the last person on board.' He pointed to a forlorn-looking man in uniform shivering in the hull. 'It's going down, so keep away.'

'No one's left on there? Really?' Carly's voice was cracked but hopeful.

'All rescued, thanks to this man and his team.'

The coastguard pointed at Owen and then waved. 'See you back at base.'

'Thank God.' Carly closed her eyes and gripped the side of the boat.

'Let's go back to help the survivors.' Noticing she was shaking, he gently peeled her hands from the metal and brought her into the cab. 'You sit down. I've got this.'

'No. Thanks.' But she leaned against him. Or had that just been caused by the sudden lurch of the boat? 'You okay, Carly?'

She pressed her lips together and nodded. 'I think so. I'm sorry. I just lost the plot there.'

'I told you, don't ever apologise for being you. I know how much you lost, Carly. I just wish I could help.'

'You do.' She smiled sadly and closed her eyes. *I love you so much. Even more now, and more each day.*

He brushed wet tendrils of hair from her face and looked at her. He was so glad to see her but worried too. 'You cut your trip short.'

'Yes. I had to come back.' She looked at her hands. He didn't want to hear her say that she'd only come back to make sure everyone was safe.

And he realised that, if he didn't want to watch her leave again, it was time to take that risk. 'Listen, I've got something to say. I need you to hear it.'

She looked up at him and frowned. 'What is it?'

He swallowed. *Jump, man. Do it.*

'I made a mistake. A huge one. I was scared about you leaving, so I did the most stupid thing and made you leave. Just to take some control and protect myself. I didn't want you to go. I thought I wasn't enough to keep you here.'

'Oh, Owen.' She cupped his face. 'You are more than enough for me.'

Was he, though? Dared he ask? He covered her hand with his. 'Truth is, I do want you to stay here, Carly. With me and Mason. But I know that's a big ask, so I'm not going to say that.'

'What?' She shook her head, no doubt confused by his rambling.

'I'm going to take Mason out of kindy, put the job here on hold and we'll come with you on your adventure. If you'll have us. Plenty of families travel. We could just do it slowly, visit all the places you wanted to explore. It'll be great learning for Mason.'

'Oh, no.' She shook her head vehemently.

His chest tightened like a vice. 'No, we can't come? No, you don't want us?'

'No, I'm not taking my boy out of kindy. He needs stability—he's only just settled in. And we both know what a rough ride he had before that.'

His heart swelled. '"My boy"?'

'Our boy.' She swallowed. 'I shouldn't have left

you when I saw how much you wanted me. But then you told me to go, and I felt rejected again.'

He'd done that? Done what all those families had done to her in the past? 'God, no. I am so sorry. I want you more than anything. I just didn't have the guts to admit it to you or myself. Until it was too late. I didn't want you to put off your plans for me.'

'I should have insisted that I stayed and made you see sense, but I was confused about how I felt. So I ran. Being alone has been my default. Sure, I had Raff for a few years, but essentially I've been on my own my whole life. I lost so much when Raff and his parents went, but I lost myself too. And I thought that if I was on my own I'd come back to me. But I know who I am, and I have to believe in myself. I have to listen to my instincts.'

'Which are…?'

'I don't need to go off on an adventure when the adventure is right here. Falling in love, growing close, building a future, building a life. The biggest risk we can take is to open our hearts, right?'

'It's been a hard lesson, but yes.' He stroked the back of his knuckles down her beautiful cheek. 'But what will you do here, if you've sold the camp?'

She shrugged. 'I'm going to take some time to

work that out. I've got a few ideas around conservation and regeneration, and I love teaching, so I might start a sustainability and nature business. Take people on tours of the island and teach them about the bush and growing native plants. We have enough visitors here now that I think I'll be busy enough. I need to do some research and get together a business plan, but the money from the camp will give me some breathing space to work out what I really want...other than being here with you and Mason. If that's okay?'

'Okay? It would make me the happiest guy alive.' He pulled her to him, just about managing to stay upright as the boat lurched from side to side.

She gripped onto his arms and looked up at him. Then he pressed his mouth to hers and kissed her, long and slowly.

When she pulled back, she was smiling, and even in the dim light he could see it: that certain sparkle he'd wanted to see. He couldn't quantify the pride he felt at putting it there. He barely had words, but he found enough. 'I love you, Carly Edwards.'

She smiled. 'I love you too. Now, let's start this adventure. Together.'

EPILOGUE

Six months later...

CARLY LOCKED THE front door of their lovely refurbished cottage and pocketed the key. Excitement rippled through her. It was really happening. 'Right, then, who has the passports?'

Owen pulled them out of his rucksack and waved them at her. 'Me. And the guidebook.'

'Excellent. I've got the money and the games for the plane.' She helped Mason put on his little carry-on backpack. 'Okay, bud. Where are we going first?'

He grinned up at her, all big, brown eyes like his dad. ''Merica, to see Mummy.'

Now, that was going to be an adventure all of its own. But Miranda had been nothing but supportive about Carly's presence in her son's life. Carly suspected that Mason having a stepmum lessened the emotional turmoil for the successful actress who still spoke to her son very regularly. Carly and Owen had made sure of it. And now Tane wasn't the only child at kindy with two mummies. They were all keen to meet up and share their love for the little boy. She ruffled his hair. 'Yup. Then where?'

'Rocky mountain.'

She giggled. 'Yes. The Rocky Mountains. For a camp out in the park. And horse riding.'

'And bears!' He pulled a face and growled.

'Hopefully not close up.' She winked at Owen. 'Lucky us. Our own adventure.'

Sure, it wasn't exactly the one she'd been planning, and it was only for the kindy holidays, but it meant more to her than any other trip she'd ever planned.

Owen pulled her close for a quick kiss. 'Did I ever tell you how much I love you for doing this? We are so lucky to have you.'

She leaned against him. She'd created a good life with the man she adored and the boy she grew to love more and more each day. 'Hey, I get to do all the things I want to do, and have you guys come along for the ride. I'm the lucky one.'

Then they jumped into the little tin boat and sped round to the harbour. To their adventure and their future. The three of them.

A family at last.

* * * * *

Look out for the next story in the
Rāwhiti Island Medics duet
Coming soon!

If you enjoyed this story, check out these
other great reads from Louisa George

Cornish Reunion with the Heart Doctor
ER Doc to Mistletoe Bride
Nurse's One-Night Baby Surprise

All available now!